PAUL'S POTTY PAGES

D0321374

Alexa Tewkesbury

Hiya. Paul here, and you'll never believe how much I've been learning about God and me in the last few weeks! Did you know that He just loves to be part of everything you do, even if you think what you're doing isn't very important? And did you realise that you might go and get yourself into a total muddle like I've just done, but He's always there to help you sort stuff out because you're so MEGA special to Him? And have you ever stopped to think that no matter what problems you've got, you don't have to get stuck dealing with them on your own because God will never leave you?

For the full story, you've just got to read my diary! It's all about me and God and my cool life with the Topz Gang. In case you haven't met us before, you can find out who we are on the next page. Being one of the Gang is definitely TOPZ. I may be short, but I'm not short on friends.

So don't hang about. Grab your goggles and dive in! See you inside …

HI! WE'RE THE TOPZ GANG

– Topz because we all live at the 'top' of something …
either in houses at the top of the hill, at the top of the
flats by the park, even sleeping in a top bunk counts!
We are all Christians, and we go to Holly Hill School.

We love Jesus, and try to work out our faith in God
in everything we do – at home, at school and with our
friends. That even means trying to show God's love to
the Dixons Gang who tend to be bullies, and can be a
real pain!

If you'd like to know more about us, visit our website
at **www.cwr.org.uk/topz** You can read all about us,
and how you can get to know and understand the Bible
more by reading our 'Topz' notes, which are great fun,
and written every two months just for you!

LIFE IS

SERIOUSLY STRANGE!

(AND IT'S ONLY MONDAY ...)

This is bad. Not just a bit bad. Or bad-ish. We are talking really bad. Mega bad. TREGA (trega?) bad! I mean, what is the matter with me? I've just turned down a treble chocolate muffin! How can anyone turn down a treble chocolate muffin? Even Mum thought I was trying to be funny. When she realised I wasn't, that I was deadly serious, she said, 'Oh, please, Paul. If you don't have it, I'll end up eating it and I've already had three.'

I said, 'Just because it's there, it doesn't mean you have to eat it.'

She glanced at me over her glasses and said, 'It does, actually.'

I said, 'Well, eat it, then.'

'No!' she said, 'I'm trying to cut down.'

'Mum,' I said, 'if you're trying to cut down, why do you buy them?' (Sometimes I do wonder who are the grown-ups and who's the child in this house.)

'Because ...' she blustered, 'I buy them for you. You usually eat them.'

I know I do, I thought. Usually. It's just that this

isn't 'usually'. I don't think anything's ever going to be 'usually' again. It's all just plain weird.

6.00pm

Been looking in the mirror. Thought I'd better check I'm still me. It looks like me. Those are definitely my glasses. There's just no way in the entire known universe it feels like me. I think I should do a test. If I pull one of my hairs out and it hurts, that'll have to mean this is me, won't it? I mean, as long as I can feel something, I must still be here. Don't fancy the idea much but sometimes you've got to take the bull by the horns – or in this case the hair by the hair shaft what's-it. Here goes … YOW! Yes, that hurt. Quite a lot, actually. I'm definitely me.

6.10pm

Shame, really. I was almost hoping I was someone else. I was thinking: if it turns out that I'm someone else today, maybe I'll be back to normal tomorrow. I liked

'normal' – messing around with the Gang, building robots out of empty yoghurt pots, seriously dodgy kickability with both feet when it comes to football. 'Normal' was nice. 'Normal' was … normal. 'Normal Paul', that's what I used to be.

Not any more.

7.00pm

Dad said, 'You're quiet.'

I said, 'Yeah.'

He said, 'Everything all right?'

I said, 'Yeah.'

He said, 'You're feeling fine, are you?'

I said, 'Yeah.'

He said, 'If there was anything worrying you, you'd tell me, right?'

I said, 'Yeah.'

He said, 'Do you want to tell me now?'

I said, 'Yeah … I mean, no.'

Trick questions. They're so sneaky.

3972   3974…

3971   3973

10.00pm

I've tried everything, but I'm still awake. I was counting sheep for over an hour. Then I tried <u>not</u> counting them, but they kept hopping into my head and going 'baa' even when I didn't want them to be there. When I got to number 3974, I had to go and stick my head under the cold tap in the bathroom.

Bad idea. My jammies are soaking and now my pillow's all wet and soggy. And cold. It's like lying on a slug.

10.15pm

Earth to brain, earth to brain. It's time to shut down.

10.30pm

I could eat that treble chocolate muffin now.

10.40pm

It's no good. I'm going to have to face up to it. 'Normal' has shot off to another galaxy and I'm left sitting in a hole on Planet Odd. Planet Wide-Awake. Planet Sheep-On-The-Brain.

10.45pm

It <u>can't</u> be. This is ME. This is Paul. I don't <u>do</u> stuff like this. I'm sensible. I invented a car wash thingy for my glasses using an empty washing-up liquid bottle and a toothbrush.

11.30pm

If I see another sheep, I'm going to scream.

11.35pm

AAAAAAAGGGHH!!

TUESDAY 14 SEPTEMBER
5.00pm

I think I'm turning into a tragic person. I spent lunch time listening to choir club. Not singing, which is why most people go to choir club. Just listening. The sad part is I even enjoyed it.

Dave said, 'Come on, we're having a goalie contest. First to ten wins.'

I said, 'No, it's all right, thank you. I think I'm going to choir club.'

Dave said, 'What for? You can't sing a note.'

I said, 'Who said anything about singing?'

He said, 'Well, why else would you go to choir club?'

I said, 'Perhaps I just want to listen.'

He said, 'Yeah. And perhaps my feet have just turned into sausages.'

I said, 'It's good to listen to music sometimes. It can be very calming.'

Dave said, 'And Mum says spinach is good for me but that doesn't mean I'm going to eat it.'

Mr Mallory said why didn't I join in with the singing instead of just sitting there.

I said, 'It's good to listen to music sometimes. It can be very calming.' He didn't say anything about spinach being good for you, though.

Sarah's doing choir club. She was in the back row. I shot off as soon as it was finished. I didn't want her asking awkward questions like: 'What were you doing at choir club?', but she caught up with me in the cloakroom.

'What were you doing at choir club?' she asked.

I said, 'Not all boys want to spend lunch time kicking a silly ball around.'

She said, 'You've never shown any interest in singing before.'

I said, 'So? Perhaps I'm trying to become a more interesting person.'

And that's when the new girl walked into the cloakroom. The new AMERICAN girl in our class. From America and everything.

'So, Taz,' said Sarah, 'what do you think of our choir club?'

Taz! Her name's Tansy but Sarah gets to call her TAZ!

'It's really cool,' Tansy said, smiling. 'Those songs are <u>so</u> great.'

It took a few moments. Then I realised.
<u>She's talking to you, you idiot!</u> This is the part where you're supposed to say something really clever and funny. You know, show her there's so much more to you than the computer nerd who tripped over her bag last week in the library and flew head first into the photocopier.

I opened my mouth. I took in a breath. I gave her what I hoped was my most un-nerdy smile. And –

'Phphleeengh!'

Sarah stared at me. She looked horrified. If I could have stared horrified at myself I would have done.

'That's … interesting,' said Tansy.

Then she was gone. Tansy Smart. The first REAL American person I've ever met. The first REAL American person ever to make me count up to 3974 sheep. The first REAL American person ever to make me <u>want</u> to

3974

give up lunch-time footie to go to choir club. The ONLY American person ever to get me to open my mouth and say, 'Phphleeengh!'

What a total **PEA-BRAIN!!**

6.00pm

I definitely need advice. Maybe I should talk to Dad. On the other hand, maybe not. Dad can be really helpful when it comes to things like homework. He knows lots about where tea comes from and how long tadpoles take to grow into frogs and that sort of stuff. He even came into school once and talked to our class about moths. Apparently he used to be quite a mothy person. Mum says that, years ago when she first knew him, he used to keep all sorts of creepy crawly things in glass jars with air holes in the lids.

Still, I can't imagine Dad being able to help with this. How's he ever going to understand what it's like sharing the same classroom with someone from America every day? I mean, we're not talking about some random place just up the road. This is the USA – massively massive and WOW! It's where <u>Star Wars</u> came from! It's the home of McDonalds! Where would the world be without the Big Mac? I am SO definitely going there one day.

No, I don't think I can talk to Dad. I need to know how to act mega cool and I just have this niggly feeling that acting cool and being mothy don't quite go together. (No offence, Dad.)

7.00pm

Perhaps I should try Greg. He's really good at being a Sunday Club leader. And I'm pretty sure he's not mothy.

Maybe he'd know how to be cool dudey-ish around someone from America.

Or I could just talk to Dad.

7.30pm

I said, 'How do you talk to someone from America without saying, "Phphleeengh"?'

Dad said, 'Why would you say "Phphleeengh" to someone from America?'

I said, 'Because America's so wicked. Imagine being from AMERICA! There is no one else that cool at Holly Hill School.'

Dad said, 'Why does being from America make you cool?'

I knew it. He's too mothy.

I said, 'Dad, think about it. She's American.'

'Right,' he said. 'Who?'

'The American girl in our class,' I exploded. Honestly, sometimes talking to Dad is like talking to a fridge magnet.

'Oh, I see,' he said finally … 'And?'

What <u>is</u> the point?

'Forget it,' I said. 'We've just got this American girl in our class, and when I try to speak to her, all that comes out is "Phphleeengh". But, who cares?'

Dad said, 'When I first met your mum, I used to talk to her about moths.'

I said, 'I don't know if Tansy's interested in moths.'

He said, 'I don't think your mum was really.'

I said, 'How come she married you then?'

He said, 'Ah. That would be my fabulous good looks and outstanding sense of humour.'

That's the trouble with Dad. I can never tell when he's joking.

12

8.30pm

When I've got a problem, I usually ask God to help me with it. Greg always says that's the best way to deal with problems. The trouble is, I'm not sure if this is a proper problem. The 'Phphleeengh' bit is sort of tricky, I suppose. But is it the kind of thing God's going to want to get involved in? He must have so much bigger things on His mind. There's Africa for a start. People in Africa need help all the time. Important help, too – not to do with saying 'Phphleeengh', obviously, but lots of them don't have anything to eat. If it was a choice between helping someone who wants to be cool dudey-ish around someone from America or helping a poor, starving person in Africa, I know who I'd choose.

8.45pm

I asked Mum, 'Will God help you with a problem even if it's a bit pathetic?'

She said, 'God doesn't think anyone's problems are pathetic. If something's big enough to bother you, it's big enough to bother Him and He'll want to help you sort it out. The thing about God is that He just loves being involved.'

I said to Dad, 'Do you ever pray about something that you feel a bit silly praying about?'

He said, 'You never need to feel silly when you talk to God. He loves you – whatever you talk to Him about.'

8.55pm

I wonder if Dad ever talks to God about moths.

9.00pm

Lord God, there's something I need to ask You. I don't know who else to talk to. As problems go, I know it's totally sad, but I'd really like to be friends with Tansy. She's from America. That means she is super cool! Her parents probably drive one of  those big cars like you see on TV. I mean, how stonking is that! Trouble is, I can't seem to talk to her. I don't know what to talk <u>about</u>. I think I'm just scared she's not going to like me. I know there are more important things, but this is important to me. Please could You help me? Help me know what to say. Anything other than 'Phphleeengh' would be great. Thanks. Amen.

9.30pm

Whatever else happens tonight, I am NOT counting sheep.

Paul, you noodle head, it's 10.30pm! Come on, sleep, sleep, SLEEEPPP!!

11.00pm

Lying in bed not sleeping is so boring. I'd yawn with boredom if I could, but I'm too wide awake.

WEDNESDAY 15 SEPTEMBER

7.00pm

Things not going well on the cool-dudey front.

We had PE and Mrs Parker wanted us to get into

fours. She loves doing that, dividing us up into groups of four. I expect it's because there are 32 of us in her class so, as long as no one's away like today, she ends up with exactly eight equal groups. She likes everything neat and tidy, I've noticed. Even her ticks in my maths book are all the same size. I bet her whole house is scarily spotless and mega well-organised. So when I tried to make up a five, she wasn't having it.

It was Josie's fault. I was just about to join Dave's group when she called out, 'Paul, over here. We've only got three.' I turned round. That's when I saw who was with her. There was Sarah, which was fine. But then there was Tansy Smart which, as fine stuff goes, was just about as UN-fine as you can get. Don't get me wrong, I mean it would have been fantastic to be in Tansy's group. Treble fantastic, even, with huge great bells on. But how can you do one of Mrs Parker's PE thingies with someone you can only say 'Phphleeengh' to? If it happens again, I'm going to have a serious problem convincing her that I am just the sort of cool dude she should be hanging around with. So I can't let it. Which means that until I've been able to come up with a brilliant plan for how to be in the same room with her and talk to her in proper words that she might actually be able to understand, the best thing I can do is to say nothing and just smile at her in a warm sort of way – if there happens to be an appropriate opportunity, that is. Obviously a warm sort of smile at the wrong moment could be as much of a disaster as saying 'Phphleeengh' again.

So anyway, Josie called out, 'Paul, over here.' I was about to join her when I spotted Tansy next to her. I started to say, 'No, it's all right, I'm with Dave,' but before I'd finished, Max appeared out of nowhere and made up Dave's four, and there I was, all alone and groupless. I wondered if Mrs Parker would notice if I slipped in behind Dave. After all, I'm smaller than he is and, anyway, four in a group, five in a group, what's the big deal? But, no. Having uneven groups was too much of a step into the unknown for Mrs Parker.

'Paul,' she said, snapping her fingers (one of those annoying, teachery things she's always doing), 'there are three girls left over here.'

'But,' I began, 'I was going to go with Dave.'

'No, no!' Her voice was as snappy as her fingers. 'Dave's already got four. Come along, chop chop.' (Whatever that means.) And that was that.

For one tiny moment I did think that perhaps this could be my chance to show Tansy that I'm actually pretty smooth and sporty. (The fact that I'm not smooth or sporty could be a bit of a problem, but at times like this you just have to think positive.) Only then Mrs Parker told us what she wanted us to do. And that's when I knew I was sunk.

'In your groups, you're going to invent a machine. I want you to use your whole bodies to be the different parts of the machine as it's working. And I want sounds – clanking, banging, whirring. Use your imagination.'

If I <u>had</u> an imagination, I suppose I could have tried to use it to get out of doing PE. As I haven't, I had to do what Josie said. It's not really her fault. She just has no idea what it's like having a hard time making friends with an American person. Making friends with anyone from anywhere always seems so easy for Josie. But,

seriously, how can you impress someone from America when you're having to pretend to be part of a machine, bouncing up and down, whirling your arms around like a demented windmill and going 'Brring-splott, brring-splott'?

I blame Mrs Parker. Teachers have no understanding of basic human dignity.

8.30pm

I was in my bedroom doing my maths homework.

Dad knocked on the door and said, 'How's it going?'

I said, 'Fine. It's just fractions. They're really not hard.'

'That's not what I mean,' he said. 'I mean, how's it going with your American friend?'

'Dad,' I reminded him, 'she's <u>not</u> my friend.'

He said, 'Well, how's it going anyway?'

I said, 'Let me put it this way. Now that Tansy's seen what I'd look like if I was a windmill with shorts on, I can't see why she'd ever want to have anything to do with me.'

He said, 'Jolly good. Keep me posted.'

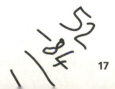

THURSDAY 16 SEPTEMBER
8.30pm
Dave came round after school so we could take him
to Boys' Brigade. We were watching TV in the lounge
and the first thing Dad did when he came in from work
was stick his head round the door and say, 'Anything to
report on the American front?'

Dave looked at me and asked, 'What's the American
front?'

I said, 'It's nothing.'

'No, really,' Dave said. 'What's the American front?'

'No, really, it's nothing,' I said.

Dave looked at Dad.

'It's nothing,' Dad said. 'Really.'

9.00pm
I said to Dad, 'Why did you have to say that in front of
Dave?'

Dad said, 'Sorry. I didn't realise it was a secret.'

I said, 'How can something be a secret when it's not
even anything?'

He said, 'Well, when it is something, let me know and
then I'll make sure not to tell anyone.'

'But it's <u>never</u> going to be something,' I said. 'I mean
I'm never going to get to be Tansy's friend.'

'Why not?' Dad asked.

'Because I'm not interesting enough,' I said. 'And
even if I was, I'm too short.'

'What's that got to do with it?' he said.

'Everything,' I said. 'If you're American and you're
going to have friends, you'd want them to be tall and
sporty, wouldn't you?'

'Not usually,' said Dad.

'But she's from America,' I said. 'Everyone's tall and sporty out there.'

'I think they're probably not, actually,' said Dad. 'Anyway, it doesn't matter what other people are like. God created a huge variety. All shapes and sizes. And when He looks at you, Paul, He's very proud of what He's made.'

'I suppose so,' I said.

'There's no suppose about it. Trust me. I know these things.'

9.15pm

Dear Lord God, I know You made me just as I am and so I should be quite happy with that because You are. But, would it be possible for me to grow just a little bit taller quite quickly – at least so that I'm the same height as Tansy, and then she won't have to look down at me when I eventually get up the nerve to talk to her? Thanks. Amen.

FRIDAY 17 SEPTEMBER
6.00pm

The most awful thing happened. The worst thing in the world.

I was walking through the cloakroom when I heard Tansy giggling with some other girls. She's got this real American giggle, too.

But then she said it. And suddenly I realised. It's not being shorter than Tansy that I need to worry about.

'I mean, can you imagine?' she was saying. 'They're so horrible. If I had to wear glasses <u>all</u> the time, I think I'd just <u>die</u>.'

6.30pm

That's it then. Tansy hates glasses. No wonder she doesn't want to have anything to do with me. She'd probably rather make friends with a yoghurt.

SATURDAY 18 SEPTEMBER
10.00am

I've been looking in the bathroom mirror. Staring, really. At myself. In my glasses. I'd still be doing it now if Dad hadn't kept banging on the door and saying things like, 'Any chance of you coming out before Christmas, Paul?' and, 'Are you having a shower or have you actually taken root?'

It's impossible to see myself without glasses. On the one hand, I just can't imagine what it would be like not to have them on my face all the time, and on the other it is actually impossible for me to <u>see</u> myself without them. When I take them off, my eyesight's so bad that my face in the mirror disappears into a murky sort of blur. I could be looking at anything – a vaguely pink and quite large ice cream sundae, for example.

I said to Sarah last night at youth club, 'Would <u>you</u> mind having to wear glasses all the time?' (Sarah can be quite kind and understanding sometimes.)

She said, 'I don't know. I've never had to wear them.'

'But if you did,' I said, 'would you worry that they made you look … I don't know … ugly?'

'It's hard to say,' she said, 'not ever having had to wear them.'

'But, if you looked at someone like, say, me, for example,' I said, 'would you think that boys who wear glasses are just SO not like tall, sporty boys who … don't?'

'I'm not really sure what you mean, Paul,' she said. 'If you need glasses, you need glasses. And you're just someone who needs glasses.'

Then she disappeared off to play table tennis with Josie. So much for kind and understanding.

Greg said, 'Everything all right, Paul?'

I said, 'Why?'

He said, 'You don't seem to be your usual madcap self this evening, that's all.'

Madcap? I never realised that's how Greg saw me.

'What is it?' he went on. 'What's up?'

'Nothing,' I shrugged. 'Nothing at all if I was the sort of person who was quite happy to have to wear glasses for the rest of his life.'

'You've never mentioned your glasses before,' he said.

'I've never really thought about them before,' I said.

'So how come they're bothering you now?'

'They're not,' I said. 'I mean, actually they are, but so what?'

Greg said, 'If you're having trouble seeing with them, maybe you should ask your mum to take you back to the optician.'

'It's not seeing with them that's the problem,' I said. 'It's being seen with them on.'

'What do you mean?' Greg smiled. 'You look great in your glasses. A real brain box.'

Madcap <u>and</u> a brain box? There's obviously more to me than I thought. (I wish.)

10.30am
Mum wears glasses.
Dad wears glasses.
I wear glasses.
We're a family of glasses-wearers.

11.00am
I said to Dad, 'Have you always worn glasses?'
He nodded. 'Since I was knee-high to a slug.'
'What about Mum?'
'I'm not sure. I think so.'
'So I've got no hope, then,' I mumbled.
'No hope of what?' Dad asked.
'<u>Not</u> having to wear glasses.'
'It's the family weakness, I'm afraid,' he said.
'Do you ever worry that wearing glasses makes you look … ugly?'
'No, I can't say I do. Most of the time I'm just glad they help me to see. I'd be lost without them.'
He did get lost without them once, I remember. In a caravan park in Devon. He put them down in the shower block but couldn't remember where, and then he couldn't find his way back to our caravan to get help because he couldn't see. Tragic really, but tummy-achingly funny at the same time.
'Is that what you think?' Dad asked. 'You think glasses make you look ugly?'
'What if I do?' I said. 'I've just got to accept it.'
'But it's not true,' Dad said. 'Glasses can give a face real character. I always think that lots of people look

much better with glasses than without them.'

Yeah yeah yeah.

He said, 'Anyway, these days they're a fashion what's-it, aren't they?'

'Accessory.'

'That's it, a fashion accessory,' he said. '<u>We</u> are a trendy family, I'll have you know.'

Wait for it. Next thing, he'll be telling me my glasses make me look like a brain box.

'And I've always thought,' he went on, 'what an absolute brain box you look in yours.'

I knew it.

'It doesn't matter,' I said. 'You can be a brain box and still be ugly.'

Dad said, 'You're <u>not</u> ugly, though. And God certainly doesn't think you're ugly.'

'But I <u>am</u>. <u>And</u> I'm short. Why did God want me to be short <u>and</u> ugly? Why couldn't I at least have had good eyes so I didn't have to wear glasses?'

11.20am

I wonder where a slug keeps its knees.

11.45am

I've decided what I'm going to do. I'm going to try to make my eyes better. It can't be that hard. I've just got to train them to work without glasses. It'll be like when John was training Gruff. When Gruff was a puppy, he didn't understand how to do anything. Now he's had loads of practice doing 'sit' and 'stay' and he can do it really well – when he feels like it. Of course, a lot of the time he pretends not to hear you. Anyway, it's just the same with my eyes. All they need is practice at seeing by themselves. Then they'll be perfect.

11.55am
Just done my first eye-training session. It was good and not so good. The good bit was that when I took my glasses off, I managed to walk nearly the whole way round my bedroom without bumping into anything. The not-so-good bit was that I've just fallen over my chair. It's the same colour as my carpet. Now I think I've broken my toe.

AAWW!!!

2.30pm
Mum turned the hoover off when I went into the lounge. She hates it if you interrupt her when she's doing the hoovering. She's got this thing about needing to finish what she's started before anything else happens. So if <u>she</u> turns the hoover off herself before she's finished, you know she must be going to say something pretty seriously serious.

'Sit down with me for a minute, Paul,' she said.
Seriouser and seriouser.
'I've been talking to Dad,' she said.
Normal mum and dad sort of stuff then.
'He says you seem bothered about having to wear glasses all of a sudden.'
Oh, right. Now I get it. This is a 'Paul, you are SO not ugly and you mustn't think of yourself as ugly' talk.
I said, 'It's not what <u>I</u> think, it's what other people think that matters.'
She said, 'Who cares what other people think? <u>What matters is what God thinks. He's made you so clever and</u>

SERIOUSER AND SERIOUSER!!!

so thoughtful and so funny and so gorgeous. Those are amazing gifts He's given to you. You need to try and concentrate on them and then maybe you'll realise how special you are to Him.'

I said, 'Will it make me more popular if I do that?'

She said, 'But you are popular. You've got friends who think the world of you. And nothing could make you more popular with God. He loves you exactly as you are because that's the way He made you.'

'People aren't like God, though,' I said. 'People look at other people and think they're ugly.'

'You're right,' she said, 'people aren't like God. God is huge and powerful and kind and loving. And if a huge, powerful, kind, loving God like that loves you just the way you are, then you have to learn to feel that way about yourself. Otherwise it's a bit like saying that what God's made isn't good enough.'

'But why do I have to wear glasses?' I said. 'None of my friends do.'

Mum said, 'God made everyone to be different. Some people have big feet, some people haven't. Some people's ears are tiny, other people's stick out. Some people are fantastic at maths like you. Others are hopeless at it like me. You happen to need glasses. So what? Just because your eyes need a bit of help doesn't make you any less special and it certainly doesn't make you ugly. You shouldn't try to compare yourself to anyone else. You're a one-off. That's how God made you. And He loves what He's made.'

3.30pm

I can see that. I really can.

But it doesn't change the fact that Tansy hates glasses.

3.35pm

I'm sorry, Lord God. I'm sorry if it looks as though I think what You've made isn't good enough. It's great, it really is. I mean, I've got arms and legs and a head and all the other stuff I need. So, thank You for everything. Could You maybe just help Tansy to see me more like You do – you know, as a one-off person rather than a blob with glasses? Thanks again. Amen.

SUNDAY 19 SEPTEMBER

9.30am

Eyesight training not going so well. Tried to do my Bible study without my glasses. Couldn't read a word.

Humph.

2.00pm

At Sunday Club Greg said, 'You're not still worried about wearing glasses, are you?'

I said, 'A bit. It doesn't matter, though. I'm going to try and learn to see without them.'

He didn't answer for a moment. I could see him thinking. He does this kind of chewy-lip thing when he's thinking.

Then he said, 'Does wearing glasses stop you being able to do anything?'

I said, 'Yes. It's stopping me being the sort of person I want to be.'

'And what sort of person's that?' he said.

'Tall and sporty.'

'Glasses aren't going to stop you being sporty,' he said. 'And who knows how tall you're going to be when you're older? Anyway, what do you think's more important to God – being tall and sporty or being the person He wants you to be?'

'It's not as simple as that, though,' I said. 'When you know people think wearing glasses is just <u>so</u> uncool, how's that supposed to make you feel good about yourself?'

He said, 'God made everyone equal. We're all totally different from each other, yes, but we're all equal. No one has the right to pick holes in anyone else.'

'It doesn't stop them doing it, though,' I said.

'I tell you what you need to do,' Greg went on in a scarily enthusiastic voice. 'This week you need to stop being so gloomy and try and focus on five fantastic things God's given you. Five really great things about yourself. You know, things you're good at, things you like about yourself, that sort of stuff. Write them down, then look at them every morning when you wake up and every night before you go to bed – and any time you feel like, in between. And every time you look at those five things, say thank you to God for them.'

'What if I can't think of five things?' I asked.

'That's not an option,' Greg said. 'Five things, that's all. And when you start looking at the really positive things about yourself, it'll help you to realise just how much you've got going for you. You, Paul, have got so much potential. You've got God in you! He's got an amazing purpose for your life. And like it says in the Bible, "nothing is impossible with God".'

4.30pm

Five great things about myself. OK. Here goes: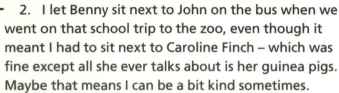

1. I'm good at maths and science. Is that a great thing? I suppose it is if I want to be a maths person or a scientist when I grow up. (Even wearing glasses could be good if I want to be a scientist. I could be one of those mad professors. I've got the right hair for it.)

2. I let Benny sit next to John on the bus when we went on that school trip to the zoo, even though it meant I had to sit next to Caroline Finch – which was fine except all she ever talks about is her guinea pigs. Maybe that means I can be a bit kind sometimes.

3. I can put on a blindfold and still tell the difference between a chocolate muffin and a double chocolate muffin. Not sure what that's about but I reckon it's something quite positive.

4. Dave picked me to work with him on the health and safety project at Boys' Brigade because he says I'm a laugh and I have lots of good ideas. (I wonder if that counts as two – brainy and good sense of humour?)

5. I can't think of a number 5 … Yes, I can. I once managed to mend one of the school computers in the lunch hour. Mrs Parker said it was wonderful to have someone technical in her class and how nice it was of me to mend a computer instead of going out to play. Perhaps I'm nice and technical.

5.30pm

Thank You, Lord God, for the good things You've put in me. Thank You for making me who I am. Help me to remember that You're always with me and that You've got an amazing purpose for my life. Amen.

5.35pm

That wasn't as hard as I thought it would be.
There is positive stuff about me. Sooner or
later Tansy's just got to start seeing it.

MONDAY 20 SEPTEMBER

7.00am

Just had the most
brain-churningly
brilliant,
megaTASTIC
idea! I woke up and
there it was in my head.
I mean, so what if my eyes need a bit
of help? I'm going to show Tansy that wearing glasses
has nothing to do with the real me. Wearing glasses
is just so squishingly NOT important when it comes
to being Paul. And it's all because of what Greg was
talking about in Sunday Club yesterday. Not the bit
about thinking up the five positive things (even though
that was really spot on and helpful and all that), but the
Bible study bit.

We were looking at this passage in the Bible
(Philippians 3:7–14). Verses 13 and 14 talk about
pressing on to win the prize God has for us, and not
looking back at our life without Him but looking
forward to our life with Him. That's when I realised.
That's exactly what I have to do with Tansy – I've got to
press on and not give up, and then in the end she'll see
that actually I'd be a fantastic person to be friends with.
After all, I'm in the Topz Gang. And we're TOPZ!

When I went to bed last night Dad said, 'You seem a
lot happier.'

I said, 'Yes, I am. We were looking at Philippians in Sunday Club and it says that we have to press on to win the prize. So that's it. I've just got to press on trying to make friends with Tansy.'

Dad didn't look too sure. Then he said, 'That's fine, Paul. I'm all for good positive thinking. But in Philippians it also says that nothing is as important as knowing Jesus. The prize we should press on towards is being with Him.'

'I know that,' I said.

'Mmm,' Dad said quietly. 'Just don't let wanting to be friends with Tansy become the most important thing. It's not as if you haven't got lots of other friends.'

I know I've got lots of other friends, I thought, but none of them are from America like Tansy, and there may never be another American person at Holly Hill School EVER again. I've got to grab the iron while the ironing needs doing – or whatever that saying is.

No, I know exactly what I'm going to do. I'm going to turn into someone tall and sporty! So, I'll work out a fitness plan. I can get Danny to help me. He's really into sport and he's good at it too. If I get fitter I'll be healthier, and if I'm healthier I'll probably get taller because everything will be working better like my heart and lungs and all that, so that ought to make me grow. Then I'll be able to be on the football team and Tansy will be SO impressed!

I'm going to plan a fitness timetable. I can do keep fit twice a day – first thing in the morning before school and then after school as well. That way I'll get fit twice as quickly. Doing it in the morning may mean I won't have time to do my Bible study then, but it'll be all right because I can do it later. That doesn't mean I'm not pressing on for God. And anyway, I'm sure He'll understand. Sometimes there are things you just <u>have</u> to do.

8.00am

Mum wanted to know what all the noise was.

I said, 'Star jumps. I've just done twenty in my bedroom.'

She said, 'Whatever for?'

I said 'It's all part of my plan. I want to be a fit kid.'

She said, 'Is it part of your plan to mend the kitchen ceiling when you come crashing through it?'

8.20am

Thought I'd better have an extra shower after all that sweaty jumping about. Now Mum says I'm late for the school bus – which is actually pretty groovy because it means I'll have to run to catch it. If I make sure I'm late every morning, that'll give me more fitness training.

Yo yo yoh!

5.30pm

Why does being fit have to be such hard work? My legs feel as if they've been holding up the roof of my house for at least the whole of my life. I've just been doing jogging round the park with Danny. When I saw him at school I said could he please help me to get fit and he said we could do some running and stuff after school. The trouble is, after I'd done the running I didn't have any energy left for the stuff (which turned out to be press-ups and scrunchy things you can do with your tummy to make the muscles stronger). Even my running was useless. Danny overtook me on every lap. Several times! When we finally stopped because I couldn't actually stand up any more, Danny must have been round about 150 times to my 5. He said (not out of breath or anything), 'Never mind, you'll get better.'

I said (hardly able to breathe at all), 'How come you've got legs and I've got two lumps of jelly?'

Danny said, 'It's just practice. Anyway, what's made you turn into a fitness nut all of a sudden?'

I managed to mumble, 'Oh, nothing in particular. Just fancied a change.' Then I had to go back to trying to breathe again.

One thing's for sure. I'm never going to be tall and sporty if I don't get fitter than this.

7.00pm

Just remembered my Bible study. Actually, I remembered it about an hour ago. But then Mum asked me if I'd like a piece of home-made flapjack because she hadn't long taken it out of the oven and it was still all warm and gooey, so I sort of needed to go and eat a bit. After all, you have to make sure you eat properly when you're doing lots of exercise. That's what Danny says. Apparently it's all about keeping your energy levels up – which is fine by me because eating is ace anyway.

8.00pm

Must do my Bible study in a minute. I've just finished my sunflower sketch for science. (If I'm honest I suppose it doesn't look much like a sunflower, but Mrs Parker set the homework so I guess she'll realise what it is.)

Now I'm going to have a go at some of those scrunchy tummy things Danny showed me. They looked pretty easy actually.

8.05pm

Awwww!!!

8.10pm
For something that looks easy, scrunchy tummy things are unbelievably hard … and I've only done three.

8.15pm
I think I've been sat on by an elephant.

8.25pm
Make that two elephants.

9.00pm
Mum said, 'You look exhausted.'
  I said, 'Yeah. I'm off to bed now.'
  Dad said, 'Good idea. Anyone would think you'd been sat on by an elephant.'

9.10pm
Dear Lord God, I know I haven't got round to doing my Bible study, even though I said I'd get round to it later. Don't worry, though. I can just do today's study when I do tomorrow's tomorrow – if You see what I mean. It's just that I've got to go to sleep now. This fitness business is REALLY tough. I don't know how fit people stay fit enough to keep fit. Amen.

TUESDAY 21 SEPTEMBER

7.30am

This is getting worse. I'm trying to do my star jumps, only every time I land, my elephant-squished tummy gets jiggled about and it's agony. Seriously. They should be called agony jumps.

7.45am

Mum said, 'Still doing your ceiling wrecking, then.'

I said, 'Yes, Mum, of course I am. Do you really think I'm the sort of person who starts something one day, then drops it the next because he's got bored?'

I was a bit miffed really. I mean, all right, I know there was that time when I was six and I gave up playing the recorder after about five minutes even though I'd been going on for ages about how much I wanted to learn it. But is it my fault I turned out to be about as musical as a dustbin? Anyway, sometimes you just have to try these things.

Getting fit's different. I really believe I can do it. And I <u>really</u> want to be cool like an American person.

8.15am

Danny just rang to say he's going swimming after school and would I like to go with him. I said, 'You bet your flippers I would!'

REMINDER: Do Bible studies as soon as you get back from swimming.

Mum's calling that if I don't get a move on I'll miss the bus. What she doesn't realise is that being late for the bus is all part of my wickedly clever keep fit plan. Anyway it's only – 8.30?? That's a bit <u>too</u> late. Oops.

4.30pm

Mum said, 'So why didn't you go swimming after all?'

I said, 'I just decided it wasn't what I wanted to do.'

Mum said, 'Wasn't Danny disappointed? It sounded as if he was really looking forward to going with you.'

I said, 'So what if he was? You can't always do things just because other people want you to. Anyway, can we not talk about this any more, please? I've got a science test to revise for.'

4.45pm

I had to get out of it in the end. Swimming, that is. Danny and I were sitting on the steps at break. He was telling me all about how to do a flip turn in the pool. Can't say I like the sound of it much. I mean, if you flip upside down in a swimming pool all the water is obviously going to shoot up your nose. Danny says it all happens so quickly that you don't notice it. I've been told that before, though, when I went on a corkscrew roller coaster with Uncle Will at this theme park we went to on holiday.

I said, 'But look at it, Uncle Will. You go completely upside down.'

'Nah!' said Uncle Will. 'Well, all right, you do go upside down, but it happens so quickly you don't notice it.'

I did notice it, though. I noticed it a lot. I was sick.

A lot.

So anyway, there I was on the steps with Danny talking about swimming stuff when Sarah walked by with Tansy.

Sarah said, 'You two going swimming, then?'

Danny said, 'Yeah. After school. I'm going to show Paul how to do flip turns.'

Sarah said, 'Eeew! I hate those. The water always shoots up my nose. Can you do them, Taz?'

Tansy said (and this was the moment I realised going swimming was a hideous mistake), 'I can't stand to swim. We have to do it at school back home. I mean, who wants to get that wet? It's just gross. And seriously UNcool.'

5.00pm

I said to Danny at lunch time, 'Danny, I've just remembered. I'm not going to be able to make swimming.'

Danny said, 'Why not? I thought you really wanted to go.'

I said, 'I did. I mean, I do. It's just … I've got some stuff I've got to do for Mum. Sorry. I forgot.'

He said, 'But your mum said you could go.'

I said, 'I know … She forgot too.'

He said, 'Right.'

I said, 'Sorry.'

He said, 'It's fine, don't worry about it. We'll go another time.'

I said, 'Yeah … well … I mean, maybe. If I'm not busy … or something. You know how it is.'

I think I got away with it. Until home time. Then I did this really stupid thing.

Tansy was in the cloakroom getting her bag.

If I don't say something now, I thought, she's going to spend the rest of her life thinking I'm a swimming geek. Worse. A swimming geek who wears glasses.

She'll hate me forever.

I <u>had</u> to talk to her. If all that came out was 'Phphleeengh', it was too bad. She couldn't think any worse of me than she did already. I'd have to chance it.

'Tasny …' I said. 'I mean, Tansy.' I was squirming.

She turned.

'I-I managed to get out of it,' I stammered.

'Out of what?' she answered.

'Swimming,' I replied. (So far, things were going really well. I was speaking in proper words.)

Tansy was looking blank.

'Danny wanted me to go swimming with him after school. I was trying to go along with him to be kind but, urgh! Swimming, eh? I mean, swimming is <u>so</u> for losers!'

'Right,' she said. 'I've got to go. Oh, and Paul, here's a tip for you: if you're going to talk about people, you might want to wait until they're not in the room.'

She ran off giggling. I turned round. That's when I saw Danny.

7.00pm

Dad said, 'What's up with you this evening?'

'Nothing,' I said.

'Still got problems with your American friend?' he said.

'Dad,' I said, 'how many times? She is <u>not</u> my friend.'

'Then why the gloom?' he said. 'It's not like you

to be gloomy.'

'I think I might have sort of upset Danny, that's all.'

'How did you do that?'

'Well, Danny was going to go swimming with me which I thought would be ace because I'd get super fit in no time. Only it turns out that Tansy can't stand swimming, so I thought I'd better get out of it otherwise she'd think I was even more of a freak than she already does. But when I told her I wasn't going swimming after all and actually I hated it too, Danny was standing right behind me. He heard every word, Dad. He said, "If you didn't want to go swimming you should have said so, instead of making me look like a total idiot."'

'Mmm,' said Dad. 'Bit of a muddle then.'

I said, 'More than a bit. I mean, I said I was sorry and I honestly hadn't meant it to sound like that, but he just sort of went off. Danny's my friend and now he hates me too.'

'Come here, dafty,' Dad said, and he put his arms round me and gave me one of his wrap-me-up cuddles. I like it when he does that. It makes me feel safe. (Not that I'd tell anyone, obviously.)

Then he said, 'You can't make people like you, you know. If you spend your time trying to be something you're not just because you think someone else doesn't like you the way you are, you're not really being true to yourself.

And you're certainly not being the person God wants you to be.'

'But I don't know who God wants me to be.'

'Yes you do,' Dad said. 'He wants you to be Paul – kind, funny, always inventing things.'

'But Tansy doesn't want a friend who invents things.'

'Then,' said Dad, 'maybe you should be concentrating on the friends you've got who like you just the way you are. Like Danny. Don't push God out because of Tansy. Life shouldn't be about fitting in with the rest of the world, trying to do what other people want because you think it makes you more popular. Life's about living for God. Doing what God wants. Being what God wants us to be.'

'I know all that,' I said, 'but God doesn't seem to want me to be anything very exciting.'

'He hasn't finished with you yet, you dope,' Dad smiled. 'He's got plans for you that you don't even know about. Anyway, He lives in you. What could be more exciting than that?'

8.30pm

Dear Lord God, I'm sorry for trying to be something I'm not. Help me to remember that You made me and You love what You've made. Help me to know that You have a real purpose for me. Why do I keep forgetting all that? And help me to keep You at the centre of my life. Because I've been thinking about Tansy all the time, I've been pushing You out. And because I've been pushing You out, I've ended up letting down one of my best friends. I'm really sorry. Thanks for listening. Amen.

Stick the keep fit. I'm going to do my Bible studies now.

WEDNESDAY 22 SEPTEMBER
5.00pm

TOPZY TURVY!!!

AM I UP?
AM I DOWN?
AM I SPINNING ROUND AND ROUND?

Bounce!   Bounce!

Tansy ONLY asked me to go to trampolining with her tomorrow evening! Me! Paul! Non-sporty dude! With my glasses and EVERYTHING!!

Well, she didn't exactly ask me, I suppose, but as good as. It went like this:

Tansy was on the grass showing some other girls how to do somersaults. I mean, <u>real</u> somersaults! Not head-over-heels whatsits or cartwheels or anything, but she actually managed to flip right over in mid-air. She was this amazing, whirly, flippy-over thing – like you see on TV! I mean, WOW!

Katie Jackson said, 'Great Scottie dogs, Taz!' (Does everyone get to call her Taz except me?) 'How do you <u>do</u> that? I'd love to be able to do that. Wouldn't you love to be able to do that?'

All the girls were nodding and I sort of said, 'Yeeaaah!' really loudly without thinking about it, and suddenly they were all looking at me – including Tansy.

I said (much more quietly), 'I mean, it must be like being a sort of spinny round bird or something.'

Silence.

'You know,' I went on awkwardly, 'flying, spinning, whizzy-dizzying, that sort of thing.'

Still silence.

I was just beginning to wish a huge, terrifying-looking fish with a massive mouth would appear out of nowhere and swallow me up, like it did with Jonah in that story in the Bible – anything to get me out of there – when Tansy spoke. To me. Well, to all of us probably, but I was there. I was one of the all of us. She had to be talking to me too.

'Come along to trampolining at the sports centre on a Thursday night. You can learn all of this stuff there.'

'Is that where you go?' I asked. (Stupid question.)

'Of course it is,' she answered. 'I've been trampolining for years but I still have to practise. So, are you guys up for it?'

She was looking round at the girls but she must have meant me as well … mustn't she?

'I'm up for it,' I said. 'I love trampolining. It's way cooler than, say, swimming, for example.'

'Right,' Tansy said.

She and the other girls sort of drifted away at that point. They were giggling about something or other, but then they're girls. You've got to expect those sorts of things. Anyway, who cares?

I'M GOING TRAMPOLINING WITH TANSY SMART TOMORROW NIGHT!

I'll be able to talk to her about what it's like being American and everything. It just doesn't get any better than this!

6.00pm

It just doesn't get any WORSE than this!

Mum said, 'But you can't go trampolining tomorrow. It's Boys' Brigade.'

6.15pm

Trying to get parents to see reason is like trying to suck up cheese through a straw – all you end up with is a red face and sore lips. Not even Dad was on my side.

I said, 'But, Dad, you know how important this is. When Tansy sees how much into trampolining I am, she's bound to think I'm cool-dudey.'

Dad said, 'And since when have you been into trampolining? I thought you were going to stop trying to be something you're not.'

'But this might be what I am,' I said. 'For all I know, underneath the curly hair and glasses, there could be an ace-tastic trampoline artist just bursting to get out.'

'But it's Boys' Brigade,' Dad said, 'and apart from anything else, aren't you in the middle of a health and safety project with Dave?'

'Well, yes,' I said (as if that had anything on earth to do with it), 'but Dave will understand. He can finish the project on his own.'

'I thought you had to do a presentation.'

'We do, but Dave can do it. He's way better at that whole standing-up-in front-of-people thing than I am, anyway.'

'No,' said Dad. 'It's not right to let someone down like that. Dave's a good friend to you. I'm sorry, Paul, but you can't go trampolining. Not on Thursdays.'

6.30pm
This is a NIGHTMARE. My ONE chance, probably my only chance EVER to do tall, sporty stuff with a tall, sporty American person, and Mum and Dad have just flattened it. Squished it to a squishy-squashy thing. Thanks, guys. Thanks a lot.

6.40pm
Mum's calling. Apparently supper's ready. Typical, that is. Mum's made supper so I'm supposed to go down and eat it. But if I want Mum or Dad to do something for me, like let me go trampolining tomorrow night, for example, I can just forget it.

Well, two can play at that game. Just because supper's ready, it doesn't mean I have to go and eat it.

6.45pm
Mum says my pizza's getting cold. What a shame –
I <u>don't</u> think.

6.50pm

Now she says she's putting it in the oven to keep warm until I feel like going down. It's going to be in the oven a very long time then, isn't it?

6.55pm

Pooh sticks. I'm hungry.

7.00pm

Actually I'm **really** hungry.

7.05pm

Been trying to distract myself from my hunger by finishing my art homework. It's not helping. I've got to colour in what I sketched in class earlier: a big bowl of fruit. Even the bananas are beginning to look like the tastiest food on the planet – and I hate bananas.

7.10pm

Found three chocolate raisins in the bottom of my school bag. Normally I wouldn't eat anything that's quite so squished and covered in fluff, but desperate times call for desperate measures.

7.15pm

Dad called upstairs.

'Are you coming down to eat this deliciously melt-in-the-mouth, four-cheese pizza your mum has spent time lovingly cooking, or can I have your bit?'

7.20pm

Dad called upstairs again.

'Mmmm. Do you know, I think your bit tastes even better than mine.'

Cheap trick.

7.45pm

OK, OK, so I went down and had supper.
But only because I felt like it, not because
they wanted me to.
Dad said, 'Great pizza, eh?'
Mum just smiled.
They think they've won.
They SO haven't.

mmm. pizza!

8.00pm

I said, 'Mum, can I ring Dave, please?'
Mum said, 'What for?'
I said, 'I just need to ask him something.'
Dad said, 'This wouldn't have anything to do with not going to Boys' Brigade, would it?'
I said, 'No, of course not. It's about … maths.'
Mum said, 'You don't usually get stuck on maths.'
'I'm not stuck,' I said. 'I just … think he might be.'
Mum said, 'Go on, then. As long as it's about maths.'
We did talk about maths.
I said to Dave on the phone, 'Have you done your maths?'
He said, 'Yes, why? Are you stuck?'
'Me? No,' I said. 'I just wondered if you'd done it.'
'Right,' Dave said.
'There is something else, though,' I said. I thought I might as well mention it as we were on the phone anyway. 'Would you mind finishing the health and safety project at Boys' Brigade on your own?'
'Why?' he asked.
'Something's come up. I don't know if I'm going to be

able to be there on Thursdays any more.'

'But we're doing it together,' Dave said. 'We agreed.'

'I know we agreed, only sometimes stuff … happens.'

'Stuff like you wanting to do trampolining with Taz, you mean,' Dave said. (Unbelievable – even Dave gets to call her Taz.)

'How did you know that?' I asked.

'Sarah told me,' he said.

'How did Sarah know?'

'Josie told her.'

'Well, how did Josie know?'

'I don't know,' Dave said. 'Does it matter?' He sounded in a bit of a moody-poody about something, if you ask me.

SARAH ⟶ JOSIE

?

'Would you <u>mind</u> if I went trampolining instead?' I said. 'It's got nothing to do with anyone else, it's just something I've always wanted to do.'

'Since when?'

'Well, since …'

'Since you heard Taz was doing it,' Dave said. 'Fine. Go trampolining. Forget our project.'

'Really? I mean, are you sure?' I said.

'I said so, didn't I?' he said.

Then he put the phone down.

Stressy, or what?

9.15pm

Dad came in to say goodnight.

I said, 'Dad, if it turns out Dave's cool about me doing trampolining instead of Boys' Brigade, please can I go?'

Dad said, 'You asked him about it on the phone, didn't you?'

I said, 'Not really. Well, maybe a bit. I mean, I might

have sort of mentioned it accidentally. He seemed fine about it, though.' Dad was wearing one of his dead serious, grown-up faces, like when we were supposed to go to Uncle Pete's for the day and he had to tell Mum there'd be a bit of a hold-up because he'd just locked the keys in the car.

'What?' I said.

Dad said, 'Mum and I have already said no to trampolining on Thursdays. Why did you phone Dave about it? You said you were going to talk to him about maths.'

'But I did talk about maths,' I said. (Well, I <u>mentioned</u> it, didn't I?)

Dad wasn't happy. 'We trusted you. I'm very disappointed, Paul.'

<u>He's</u> disappointed? What about me? <u>I'm</u> the one who's not allowed to go trampolining just because it happens to clash with something I've been doing for the last 103 years, and it really wouldn't matter if I went and did something completely different for a change.

9.25pm
All I want is a life. Is that so much to ask? I mean,

WHAT IS THEIR PROBLEM??

THURSDAY 23 SEPTEMBER

4.30pm

Josie said, 'You all fixed up to go trampolining with Taz, then?'

I said, 'How come you know about it?'

'Sarah told me,' she said.

'Well, how come Sarah knows?' I said.

'John told her,' she said.

'And what's it got to do with John?'

'Dave was talking to him,' she said. 'He's not very happy with you, actually. Can't say I blame him.'

'What are you on about?' I said.

'Dave thinks you dumped Boys' Brigade just so you can show off to Taz how great you are at trampolining,' Josie said.

Huh??

'That is <u>not</u> why I want to go trampolining,' I said. 'I just want to do something different, that's all. What's wrong with that?'

'Nothing,' she said, 'if you don't mind letting your friends down so you can go and show off.'

I was starting to get cross. I mean, what is it with everyone and me going trampolining? I could feel myself getting hotter and hotter and I had this horrible feeling my face was turning into a cherry tomato.

Josie said, 'Paul, you've gone bright red!'

Yup. Cherry tomato face. Extra ripe.

'For your information,' I said through my redness, 'not that it's any of your business, I'm not going trampolining with Taz … Tansy … whatever she's called! I've got more important things to do like finish my health and safety project with Dave at Boys' Brigade.'

'That's not what Dave thinks,' Josie said. 'And what

JOSIE

SARAH

JOHN

with upsetting him _and_ Danny, I think you're being really selfish.'

'I haven't upset Dave,' I said. 'And anyway, why would I give up Boys' Brigade? You know what's really great about Boys' Brigade? There aren't any stupid girls!'

5.00pm
I said to Dave at break, 'I'm not going trampolining so I'm all set to do the project tonight.'

Dave said, 'Oh.'

I said, 'So, I'll see you there later.'

Dave said, 'I don't know.'

I said, 'What do you mean? Aren't you going?'

Dave said, 'Of course I'm going. It's just – I think I'd rather finish it on my own.'

I said, 'But why? We're working on it together.'

Dave said, 'That's what _I_ thought, but then you suddenly weren't interested and … I think I'd rather work with someone who really wants to do it, that's all.'

5.30pm
What am I going to do? How did everything end up being this complicated? I used to spend my time inventing things and doing science experiments. You know, seeing what I could make out of lolly sticks, and taking things apart to find out how they work. Like clocks. Taking them apart's easy. It's putting them back together again that's the problem. I usually end up trying to hide all the bits and pieces in a box under my bed and then hope no one'll notice the empty space on the kitchen wall or the gap on the mantelpiece. (They always do though.)

I don't know what's happened. My life used to be all about nerding around.

Now it just seems to be about upsetting people.

5.45pm

I wonder if Dave meant it about not finishing the project with me. I think it's a bit off if he did. I mean, I did say I'd do it with him after all because I wasn't going trampolining. What else does he want?

9.00pm

Greg said, 'What's up with you two this evening? You're normally the life and soul of Boy's Brigade.'

Dave said, 'You'd better ask Paul.'

Greg asked me. I told him.

I said, 'It's Dave's fault. I nearly couldn't come tonight because of … something else, so I asked him if he could finish the health and safety project on his own. He said, "Yes, fine," only now that I <u>can</u> be here, he doesn't want me to work with him.'

Dave said, 'Go on. Tell him what the "something else" was.'

'It doesn't matter,' I said.

'It so does,' he said.

'Hold on a minute,' said Greg. 'I don't think I'm getting the full picture here.'

Dave looked right at me and said, 'That's because Paul hasn't told you how he'd rather be trampolining with his friend from America than finishing his health and safety project with me. Just because he thinks being with someone from AMERICA is so cool.'

He said it loud enough for the whole hall

to hear. I think the whole hall did hear. It all went dead quiet and everyone was staring at me.

'Come and have a chat,' said Greg.

'Why am I the one who has to have a chat?' I said. 'Why don't you want to have a chat with Dave?'

'I'll have a chat with Dave later. Right now, I want to talk to you.'

We went into his office.

'What's going on, Paul?'

There's something about the way Greg says, 'What's going on?' that makes you have to tell him. Not in a bad way. In a really good way. You somehow know that you can trust him and he won't make you feel stupid. Not like when you talk to Mr Mallory at school, for example. You know Mr Mallory's going to make you feel stupid before you even open your mouth.

So I told Greg everything. All of it. After all, it wasn't my fault Dave was having a moody fit with me. That was his fault. Totally his. Completely and absolutely. No shadows of doubts or anything.

'You see?' I said. 'It's not me, is it, it's him.'

Greg said, 'Do you know what I think this might be all about?'

'Yes,' I said, as patiently as I could but, honestly, sometimes grown-ups do ask the dumbest questions. Even Greg, apparently. 'It's about me wanting to do trampolining and being made to feel I shouldn't.' I mean, duh.

Greg said, 'Nah, I don't think that's quite it, actually. How are things between you and God?'

I mean, as if that had anything to do with it!

I said, 'This has got nothing to do with me and God. Me and God are fine.'

'The thing is,' Greg said, 'God says, "I've got you and I'm not letting go. You keep your eyes fixed on Me and together we're really going to go places." But, there's this bit inside all of us that wants us to think it knows better than God. It's always trying to say, "Hey! You don't need Him. You can run your own life, make your own decisions."'

'But it was only trampolining,' I said. 'I didn't think it was that big a deal.'

Greg said, 'It wasn't. Everyone's allowed a night off from Boys' Brigade now and again.'

'Try telling that to Dad.'

'I think what your dad may have meant is that sometimes, when we really want something, we'll do anything to get it. That's not always a bad thing. It's good to be determined and to go for what you want. Where it starts to go wrong is when the something we really want comes between us and God. When that happens, it's our selfish side that takes over. We can only think about what <u>we</u> want, not about how it might affect the people around us

– even if getting what we want means hurting others or letting them down.'

I COULDN'T BELIEVE IT!!!!!

This was so <u>not</u> my fault but somehow it was turning <u>into</u> my fault.

'Do you mean Dave? You think I've let Dave down?' I said.

'I think Dave might be feeling a bit let down, yes. After all, you had already agreed to work on the health and safety project together,' Greg said. 'And then your parents probably feel a bit let down too because they said no to trampolining, but you still tried to find a way to go.'

I didn't say anything. What was the point? Greg was the one with all the words.

He gave me one of his Greggy grins. 'It's all right, you know, you don't have to look so miserable. We're all the same. We all want what we want. It's just that, when we know about God, we have to try incredibly hard to trust Him and to believe that what He wants for us is so much better than what we could ever want for ourselves.'

Fish cakes! This conversation was just not going my way.

'Did you do what I said at Sunday Club?' Greg suddenly asked. 'Did you write down five positive things about yourself?'

I nodded – although just at that moment I didn't think I'd be able to think of anything positive about myself ever again.

'When you go home,' Greg said, 'have another look through them and think about the fantastic plans God's got for you. He wants to do such great things with your life. All you have to do is stay close to Him and, bit by bit, He'll show you what He's got in mind.'

I said, 'But supposing God's plans for me aren't the plans I want?'

Greg said, 'Let me tell you something. A long time ago – before you were even born probably – I wanted to be a doctor. For a lot of the time I was growing up that was my big plan for myself. I was going to be a famous doctor. I was going to work in a huge hospital. I might even get to travel the world visiting all the people who were ill so that I could make them better. I'd have a white coat and my own stethoscope. I think I wanted the stethoscope more than anything. But, for one reason and another, it didn't work out. I was quite angry at the time. I said to God, "You know how much I wanted this. How could you let me down?" But, you know what? God didn't let me down at all. He just had a different plan. A much better plan.'

'What was that, then?' I said.

'To do this, dopey!' Greg answered. 'To be a youth leader. You see, God knows me better than I know myself. He knew I probably wouldn't have been very happy as a doctor, stethoscope or no stethoscope. But He was absolutely sure I'd have a great time being a youth leader. And He wasn't wrong.'

'Is that what I'm supposed to do, then,' I said, 'just wait and see what God wants for me?'

'You don't have to sound so gloomy about it,' Greg

grinned. 'What God wants is for us to keep talking to Him and listening to Him. Let Him guide you. And if He ever doesn't seem to want the things you want for yourself, don't get angry, get excited! Think, "Wow! I wonder what God's planning for me instead?"'

Before we went home, I said sorry to Dave. I hadn't meant to let him down. He said it was OK. I think it is. I hope it is.

9.20pm

I'm sorry, Lord. I'm sorry I keep trying to run my life without You. I'm sure my ideas aren't better than Yours. I just sometimes wish I knew what Yours were. Amen.

9.30pm

I've got this picture in my head – Greg in a white coat with a stethoscope round his neck. It's not really a good look for him. God's right. Greg's got to be the world's best youth leader.

 Totally cool and DEFINITELY dudey!

FRIDAY 24 SEPTEMBER

7.30am

I haven't got that hunky-dunky feeling. It's Friday. It's almost the weekend. I've said sorry to Dave. I've said sorry to God. I'm going on a cycle picnic with the Gang tomorrow. I should be feeling so much hunky-dunkier than this.

4.45pm

I think I've got it! I think I know why I don't feel hunky-dunky. I worked it out in science. Mind you, I got in trouble.

Mrs Parker said, 'Paul, if you want to sit around staring into space, can you please do it in your own time and not when we're supposed to be measuring sunflowers.'

I wanted to say, 'I am not staring into space, actually, I'm thinking.'

I didn't, though. I mean, you can't, can you?

Instead, I said, 'Sorry, Miss,' and made it look as if I was joining in with the sunflower measuring even though I was still thinking. I couldn't stop. My brain just kept ticking over and over. I suddenly realised what my lack of hunky-dunkiness was all about. It's because of the people I've let down. First there was Danny about going swimming, then there was Mum and Dad, then there was Dave, and I keep letting God down because I keep pushing Him out. I've said sorry to everyone, but I still haven't got that Friday hunky-dunky buzz. It's as if just saying sorry isn't good enough.

So, anyway, now I've got a plan. I'm going to make it up to all the people I've upset by doing LOADS of good stuff for them. That way I can make it up to God too. I've already started. Danny was on cloakroom tidy-up at lunch time.

I said, 'Don't worry, Danny. I'll do tidy-up for you.'

He said, 'Why? You don't have to.'

I said, 'I know, I just want to.'

Then, later on in art, Mrs Parker asked Dave to go and wash all the glue pots out. Real gunky job that is.

I said, 'It's all right, Miss, I'll do it.'

Mrs Parker said, 'Thank you, Paul, that's very helpful.'

Dave didn't look as though he thought I was being helpful. He looked as though he thought I was being weird.

At home time he said, 'Are you all right, Paul? Since when have you enjoyed washing out glue pots?'

I said, 'I don't. I just thought it would save you doing it.'

'Right,' he said. He still looked as if he thought I was being weird.

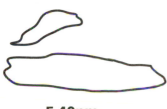

5.40pm

I said to Mum after supper, 'I'll wash up.'

She said, 'Really?'

I said, 'Yes.'

She said, 'Why would you want to do that?'

I said, 'I just want to be helpful.'

She said, 'You've never wanted to be helpful before.'

Parents. They don't make it easy, do they?

9.00pm

After youth club, Greg went and got the hoover to do the hall floor. Dad was waiting for me but I said I'd just be a minute because I wanted to help Greg clear up.

Dad said, 'Washing up? Clearing up? What are you after?'

What is wrong with the world? Can't I be a bit helpful without everybody thinking I'm up to something?

9.30pm

Dear Lord God, I'm trying to put things right. Have You noticed? Everyone's been giving me seriously strange looks. They probably think I fell out of a tree on my head this morning or something, but <u>You</u> know why I'm doing it, don't You? I'm going to do lots of good deeds for people so You'll be really pleased with me. Then all that stuff about me pushing You out because of trying so hard to get Tansy to be my friend won't matter any more, will it? And, You and me, we'll be OK again, won't we? I really want us to be OK again. Amen.

SATURDAY 25 SEPTEMBER
9.00am

It's not raining. Topz cycling trip's on. We're all meeting up with Greg at the sports centre then heading off for the old railway track. It makes a stonking cycle path because it's flat where the railway lines used to be. I can't do hills. Well, I can, but what's the point when we've got this stonking flat cycle path that's just SO much less effort?

10.00am

Mum said, 'What would you like in your picnic?'

I said, 'Don't worry, I'll do it.'

Mum said, 'You actually want to make your own picnic?'

I said, 'Yes. What's wrong with that?'

'Nothing,' she answered. 'It's just not like you to want to help out in the kitchen. In fact I sometimes think you don't know where the kitchen is.'

Here I am trying my socks off to put things right and this is the thanks I get. There's just no pleasing some people.

11.00am

Went and got my bike out of the shed. It's a bit cobwebby. I haven't used it since … the last time I used it, I suppose. It's all a bit of a jam in our shed. I was trying to lift my bike round the compost bin when there was this scary sounding crack. The next thing I knew, a shelf loaded with paint pots and all sorts of other stuff that smells incredibly bad came crashing down, missing my head by a fraction of a millimetre. Probably even less than that. I looked around. I thought, I couldn't have made this much mess if I'd done it on purpose.

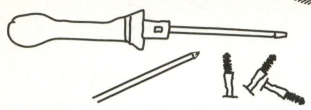

Mum and Dad heard the noise and came rushing out.
I said, 'Whoops.'

Dad said, 'Oh.'

Then his face lit up. I'm not joking, he looked absolutely over the moon. Batty or what?

'Paul!' he said. 'My man, you are a genius!'

I looked at Mum. She obviously thought he'd flipped.

Dad bent down, reached into the heap of tins and all the rest of it that had completely blitzed the floor and pulled out an adjustable screwdriver. He waved it in the air excitedly, as if it was something he'd won in one of those mega-boring crossword competitions he's always doing, and cried out triumphantly, 'Have you any idea how long I've been looking for this? Months! Months and months!'

Do all dads turn into scarily mad people eventually, or is it just mine?

I said, 'Do you want me to clear up the mess before I go cycling?'

'No,' he said. 'Don't even think about it, Paul. You've done more than enough.'

Mmm.

8.00pm

Ace, ACE DAY!!!

Well, actually there was one annoying thing. Benny was late turning up with his bike, and while I was waiting outside the sports centre with all the Topz plus some of the others from youth club, guess who had to go and arrive? Tansy Smart.

Sarah said, 'Hi, Taz. What are you doing here?'

Tansy said, 'Gymnastics.'

Wow. She does gymnastics as well. Is there anything American people aren't good at?

Josie nudged me and said, 'Still coming cycling are you, Paul?'

'Yes,' I said, 'why wouldn't I be?'

'No reason,' she said. 'I just thought you might rather be doing gymnastics.'

Ha-de-ha-ha.

Apart from that, though, everything's groovy. I mean, the good deed thing is going fantastically well. Not only was Dad knocked out by the results of my shed wrecking (which I must admit was slightly on the unexpected side), but I also got to help Danny when we were cycling because he fell down a hole. Well, he didn't exactly fall down a hole. He sort of crashed into a hole in the path on his bike and flew head first over the handlebars. It was wicked! He did this complete somersaulty thing just like Tansy was doing at school, only his landing wasn't so good. Everyone was well impressed.

I said, 'Can you try that again in slow motion?'

Greg said Danny was lucky he didn't break anything.

I said, 'He <u>has</u> broken something. His bike.'

When we looked, the front wheel was all wonky

and the tyre had a puncture. Greg said there was no point mending it, not with the wheel being bent, and we'd have to go back.

I said, 'No, we won't. Danny can ride my bike and I'll sit on the handlebars.'

Greg said, 'I'm not sure I like the sound of that.'

'It's all right,' I said, 'I've done it before.'

Danny wanted to give it a go, and in the end Greg said we could try it for a bit to see how we got on, but only if we promised to ride slowly and to get off once we were back on the road. So we locked Danny's bike up and left it down the slope in the trees to pick up on our way back. To start off with we were kind of wobbly, but once we got the hang of it, I think Greg was quite impressed. He still wouldn't let us go fast, though.

There was one drawback. If you spend too long balancing on bicycle handlebars, you do tend to get a bit sore in the sitting-down department. To be honest, I think it's one of the most uncomfortable things I've ever done and definitely something to be avoided ... Definitely definitely ... ouch ...

When we got back Danny said he'd had a great time, and Greg said it was very kind of me to put up with a sore sitting-down department so that I could help out a friend.

I said, 'It's fine. I'm putting things right. I mean, what's a sore sitting-down department compared to feeling that everything's hunky-dunky again?'

Greg said, 'What do you mean?'

I said, 'Nothing. It's between me and God, really. If that's OK with you.'

OOO

OUCH!

9.30pm

Just had a long bath. Mum thought the warm water might help my soreness of sitting down. It didn't.

10.00pm

I said, 'Night night, Mum.'

Mum said, 'Yes. Glad you had a good day.'

She seemed a bit quiet so I asked, 'Is everything all right?'

She said, 'Oh yes. Well, everything's all right with me. I'm not so sure about your dad, though.'

'Why not?' I said.

'It's that adjustable screwdriver,' she said. 'He's spent all day going round the house tightening things up.'

I smiled sympathetically. There wasn't a lot I could say. So that's what I said. Not a lot.

SUNDAY 26 SEPTEMBER

9.30am

Things still not good in the sitting-down department. I can't even seem to walk properly. I'm having to sort of waddle with a limp. Oh well. At least it's not a school day. It would be seriously bad news if Mr Mallory saw me walking like this.

3.00pm

At Sunday Club Greg said, 'Can we have a chat?'

I said, 'What, another one? Didn't we do that at Boys' Brigade?'

He said, 'Sit down a moment.'

I said, 'Do I have to?'

He said, 'Why? Are you still very sore?'

I said, 'No. Only all the time.'

HH!

AARRGH! AWWW!

Greg said, 'I've been thinking about what you said yesterday. You know, about putting things right. You do know that you don't have to work at getting God's forgiveness, don't you?'

'I'm not,' I said.

'Because, you see,' Greg went on, 'God loves us just the way we are. He accepts us just the way we are. And He forgives us just the way we are.'

Whenever Greg talks to me lately, I get this feeling my head must have turned into a groovy-shaped computer screen or something, with all my thinking processes flashing up on it. How else could he keep being right about what's going on in my brain?

'I just felt really bad about pushing God out,' I said, 'so I thought that if I did a few good deeds for the people I'd upset, they'd be happy with me again and God could forgive me more easily.'

'God forgives you anyway,' Greg said. 'Forgiveness isn't something we earn. It's not about doing ten good deeds for every one bad thing we do to make everything right again. Jesus died so that all the things we do wrong could be wiped away and we could be close to God again. What we have to do is say sorry to Him for the bad things and mean it. Forgiveness isn't about what we do for God. It's about what God's already done for us. He gave us Jesus.'

3.15pm WOW

3.30pm

TRIPLE **WOW!**

5.00pm

Dear Lord God, I hope You don't mind if I lie down to say this prayer, only sitting is slightly on the painful side at the moment. Thank You for giving us Jesus. I'm not going to stop doing good deeds. Helping people out's fun and I want to do it lots. Anyway, helping each other is what You want us to do. But I am going to stop worrying that I haven't done enough good things to make You forgive me and love me, because what would be the point? You forgave me for everything the moment I said sorry. And You love me every day. Thank You for all of that. Thanks for giving us Jesus. You're amazing. Amen.

MONDAY 27 SEPTEMBER
5.00pm

CALL ME TAZ!!

I don't get it. I just totally, completely, FRUITYFLUTELY DO NOT GET IT!! Tansy hasn't wanted to know me, certainly hasn't wanted to be friends with me and <u>definitely</u> hasn't shown any interest in anything that might be going on in my life. In fact, she SO hasn't seemed to notice me half the time that I've been beginning to wonder if I'm really here at all.

Then this morning, before school's even started, she goes and says, 'Hi, Paul. How was your cycle ride?'

I was still in the cloakroom. I hadn't even got my coat off. The worst of it was I couldn't speak. I wanted to. More than anything. I just sort of couldn't. Mum had put one of her super-chunky homemade flapjacks in my lunch box for break. Only, knowing it was in there and having to wait for break time to eat it somehow didn't go together, so I'd just taken this massive bite. I must have looked like a hamster with its pouches all stuffed up, but much scarier. Luckily Tansy couldn't see my face. I was facing my peg. I thought, if I turn round now, she'll scream or faint or run away or do whatever else girls do when they find themselves nose to nose with something hideously hideous.

So I did the only thing I could think of. I stayed with my back to her so she couldn't see my hamster pouches and gave her a thumbs up – with both thumbs, just to make it look really positive and enthusiastic.

Silence.

What I really needed to do was say something. But even if I tried, with my mouth that full of flapjack, I knew Tansy wouldn't understand a word. We'd be back to the 'Phphleeengh' situation, only worse – it would be 'Phphleeengh' with the added, highly probable embarrassment of spraying sticky, oaty lumps all over her in the process.

'Paul,' she asked after a moment, 'are you OK?'

I did the next only thing I could think of. I wiggled my thumbs. How desperate is that?!

'Great,' she said, although this must obviously have been one of the least great conversations she could have had since she'd arrived in England. 'Maybe you'll tell me about it later.'

Phphleeengh Phphleeengh Phphleeengh

Please go away, I found myself thinking.

How many Mondays start off like this? The American person you've SO been wanting to make friends with, because she's from the coolest country ever, talks to you – actually talks to you – without you having to say or do anything first, and all you can do is wish she'd go away. I don't think I'll ever be able to look at Mum's flapjack in quite the same way again.

6.00pm

Dave rang.

He said, 'How's it going with your science?'

I said, 'Fine. Really good.' (Not true. It's impossible to revise for a science test when all you can think about is why someone who doesn't even seem to like you would suddenly start getting all talky-talky with you – even when the test is about magnetism and you've been doing some funky experiments in class with magnets and paperclips.)

'Only I was wondering,' Dave said, 'could I come round for a bit and we could maybe test each other?'

'Great idea,' I said.

More time to talk, less time for thought – about Tansy that is.

The REALLY annoying thing is that I had pretty much stopped thinking about her. After all, there must be plenty of other Americans floating around. One day I'm bound to meet another one. I could actually go to America when I'm old enough. There'll be loads of them there.

Not only that, but I've been feeling OK with God again. I've made it up with everybody. I've even started to think of my glasses as a truly lovable part of my

personality no matter what Tansy thinks about them.
But then she has to go and ruin it all by suddenly
wanting to be my best friend. I mean, how is my head
supposed to deal with this? I'm a computer freak. I
don't understand girls.

6.10pm

I think I could have coped with all of it – the 'Hi, Paul' in
the cloakroom, the 'Come sit with us' at lunch time, the
'Wow! You've done such a cool Powerpoint demo!' All
that was OK. Weird, but OK.

No, it was the last bit that really got to me. There
I was, minding my own business at home time, when
Tansy breezed past and said, 'See you tomorrow, Paul.
And, hey, call me Taz. Everyone else does.'

Last week she hardly noticed me. This week she
wants me to call her Taz. I mean, WHAT IS GOING
ON HERE? I wonder if all American people are this
complicated.

8.00pm

Dave's dad just picked him up.

I never realised before what a fantastic TV quiz person Dave the Rave would make. Not a contestant, although he'd probably be really good at that too if he got asked the right things. No, he'd be amazing as the person who actually asks all the questions. He is SO ace at it. His magnet questions were spot on.

I said, 'Dave, have you ever thought about being one of those TV quiz question-askers?'

He said, 'No. I think I'd like to work in a bike shop.'

I said, 'But, Dave, you're a natural with the question-asking thing. You've obviously got unexplored question-asking talent. The question you should be asking yourself is, "Do I really want to spend my life in a bike shop when I could be famous and on the telly?"'

Dave said, 'I'm into bikes, though. Anyway, I think we ought to get back to this magnet stuff.'

Talk about wasting your talents.

Dave said, 'Name me one object that would be attracted to a magnet and one object that wouldn't.'

I said, 'You see? Question-asking genius that is.'

He said, 'I'd still rather work in a bike shop. What's the answer?'

I said, 'Ummm … a feather wouldn't and … a baked bean can would.'

He said, 'Nice one, Paul. You've just won a year's supply of marshmallows.'

If only.

Then we got on to asking each other about why magnets sometimes push each other apart and why they sometimes pull together. The trouble is, <u>that</u> got me thinking about Tansy again. I mean, why is it that last week she didn't want to know me, but this week she's being all hyper-friendly?

I said, 'Dave, do you understand girls?'

He said, 'I don't really spend much time thinking about them, and anyway, what have girls got to do with magnets?'

I said, 'What have girls got to do with anything other than mushifying your brain?'

He said, 'Is this about Taz again?'

'No,' I said. 'Well, yes. I don't know what it is but she's been so nice to me today.'

'Really?' Dave said in a definite eyebrows-raised-in-surprise way.

'You don't need to make it sound so unbelievable,' I said.

'Sorry,' Dave said.

'It's just,' I said, 'I don't want this stuff in my head all the time. I've got more important things to think about like … how I can persuade Dad to let me dig a hole in the garden so we can have a fishpond. I mean, <u>why</u> is she suddenly being so nice to me? It's all too confusing and it's making me very hungry.'

'Here,' Dave said, holding out a bag. 'Have a jelly baby.'

8.30pm

I think Dave and I ought to do all right in that science test tomorrow. We must have covered just about everything there is to cover on magnets. Glad it's not a test on what goes on inside girls' heads. The magnet stuff's SO much easier to understand.

9.00pm

Dear Lord God, Dave says that even if it's a good thing that's bothering us, we should still talk to You about it. And he should know. He's been Your friend for longer than I have. He's been talking to You about stuff for yonks. It's this whole Tansy business again. It's great she's talking to me but, basically, why is she talking to me? She thinks I'm a nerd. It's obvious. I mean, is she my friend or isn't she my friend? More to the point, should I call her 'Taz' or not? Sometimes, Lord, I wish my brain had an off switch. Thanks for listening. Amen.

9.15pm

'Feeling sleepy?' Dad asked.

'Kind of,' I said. (Not at all, actually.)

'So,' he went on, rubbing his hands together excitedly, 'where do you want your bookshelves?'

'My what?' I said.

'Your bookshelves,' he said. 'I thought you could do with a couple in here.'

'Why?' I said. 'I've got a bookcase.'

'What, that old thing?' he laughed. 'We can scrap that. What you need is some proper, solid shelves on the wall. Have a think about where you'd like them.'

'OK,' I said, 'but not tonight.'

'Why not?' he said.

'I've got a science test tomorrow.'

'Ah,' he said, a bit disappointedly. 'Just let me know by the weekend, then.'

I've never really thought of Dad as a do-it-yourself freak before. But then I suppose he's never lost a really expensive adjustable screwdriver for months and then found it again before.

TUESDAY 28 SEPTEMBER

8.00am

I said to Mum, 'Mum, can you persuade Dad that I really don't need any bookshelves in my bedroom?'

'I doubt it,' she said. 'He's gone shelf mad. He's putting one up in the bathroom later. For nick-nacks, he says.'

'What are nick-nacks?' I said.

'Bathroomy bits and pieces,' she said.

'But we've got a bathroom cabinet for bathroomy bits and pieces,' I said.

She said, '_I_ know that and _you_ know that. But this is your father we're talking about.'

4.30pm

Had lunch with Taz. Well, I suppose it was more that she had lunch with me. Dave and I were on one of the picnic benches outside, swapping crisps and talking about our health and safety project (we've got to do our presentation on Thursday), when she came and sort of plonked herself in between us. You should have seen the look on Dave's face!

'So,' she said, 'who wants to share their lunch with me?'

It was one of those totally awkward 'Are you being serious?' moments. You don't want to ask, 'Are you being serious?' in case the person is dead serious and gets a bit miffed that you thought they might be joking. On the other hand you don't want to give away your lunch.

I waited to see what Dave would do. He didn't do anything. He was obviously waiting for me. It was all too quiet.

'Sorry, I've eaten most of it,' I said finally. 'You can finish my crisps if you want.'

I could sense Dave glaring at me. I made sure I didn't look at him. When I held out the nearly empty bag, Tansy took it straight away.

'So, um, Taz,' I went on (it just sounds sad when I call her 'Taz', but hiddly-hum), 'did you leave your lunch at home?'

'Did I ever!' she said, between munching on crisp crumbs. 'Mom said I had to have school dinners. She can be so cruel. I mean, have you seen what they're serving up in there today?'

'No,' I said, 'what is it?'

'Beats me,' she said, 'but anything with that many lumps has got to be a no no.'

That was when a football came flying out of nowhere and bounced off the picnic table knocking my lunch box flying. My yoghurt spoon disappeared down a drain.

'Oops!' said Benny, bouncing over almost as out of control as the ball. 'Fantastic kick, slightly wrong direction. Sorry about that. Anyway, you lot still eating?'

'We <u>were</u> talking about our health and safety project,' Dave said, 'but I think we've finished.'

'Time for footie, then,' said Benny. 'You coming?'

'Yup,' said Dave.

They were both looking at me. So was Tansy.

'I'll … be there in a minute,' I said. Well, I couldn't go straight away. Tansy had only just sat down. It would have been a bit off to leave her there on her own.

'OK,' said Benny.

Dave didn't say anything. He didn't look happy, though.

5.15pm

I did <u>mean</u> to tell Tansy that I couldn't go to the sports centre and watch her groovy trampolining demonstration on Sunday morning because that's when I go to church, I really did. I meant to say those exact words. 'I can't because I go to church.' But somehow I just sort of didn't.

I go to church

Tansy said, 'It's such a shame you can't come trampolining on Thursday evenings.'

I said, 'Yeah, I know.'

She said, 'What is it you do on a Thursday?'

'Nothing much,' I said. 'It's just a club.' (Well, it was all right to say that, wasn't it? Let's face it, she's not likely to be interested in what goes on at Boys' Brigade anyway.)

'What kind of club?' she said. (OK, so she <u>thinks</u> she's interested, but she SO won't be if I tell her.)

'Oh, you know, just something I've been doing for ages. Mum and Dad don't want me to give it up.' At this point, I rolled my eyes in a real, 'Parents, eh? Aren't they just so out of touch with what's going on in the real world?' kind of way. I thought, I can't tell her about Boys' Brigade. It's to do with church. If I tell her about going to Boys' Brigade, it means I'll have to tell her about going to church and I don't think we know each other well enough to talk about that stuff yet.

'Well,' she said, 'you could come along this Sunday morning instead of on Thursdays. I'm doing a demonstration. On the trampoline. Oh, it's not just me, there's a whole bunch of us. It's going to be real fun, you should come.'

'Sunday?' I said. 'I … er …'

'Don't tell me you do a club then, too?'

'No. I just don't think I can make it this Sunday.'

'Why?' she said. 'What are you doing that's <u>so</u> much more important than watching me on the trampoline?'

'Nothing,' I said. 'I mean, something obviously, otherwise I could be there. I'd love to watch you on the trampoline. It's just … I'm … going to be out with my parents. Somewhere.'

5.35pm

I don't know why I didn't tell her. I should have just come out with it. 'I go to church.' That's all I had to say. But somehow, sitting there, with her looking right at me (and being able to understand every word I was saying because, rather scarily, everything coming out of my mouth was making perfect sense), I couldn't. We were having a chat. Just like friends do. Proper friends.

 Only, Tansy – she's AMERICAN! Someone from America was treating me like one of her mates and not some crazy person with dodgy eyesight. If I told her I go to church, she might get the wrong idea about me.

I mean, I'm really glad I go to church, and being God's friend is totally cool, but what if Tansy doesn't see it that way? I don't want her thinking I'm some sort of weird goody-goody. Especially now she's actually started talking to me. After all, I'm not a goody-goody. I'm always getting things wrong. Not that I'm naughty all the time, I don't mean that, but I just think Tansy needs to know me a bit better before she finds out that sort of stuff about me. About being God's friend. She needs to know what a laugh I can be – you know, zany but with a hint of braininess, when in the right mood. That's all right, isn't it? That must be how everyone feels. I bet even Dave the Rave finds it hard to tell people about God sometimes. I'm sure he does. Positive, in fact. And in lots of ways I'm just like Dave.

Telling other people about God and what He means to you isn't always that easy.

8.00pm

Benny rang.

He said, 'Are you testing out for the inter-school quiz challenge on Friday?'

I said, 'You bet your ear plugs I am!'

I've been waiting for this for ages! Six local schools enter the quiz but you only get the chance to be on the team when you're in our year. To give Holly Hill the best chance of winning, Mrs Parker organises a written question test for anyone who wants to have a go. A bit like an audition, I suppose. Then she picks the team members from the ones who know the most answers. Last year our school came second.

I said to Benny, 'Why? Are you doing it?'

He said, 'Yeah, but I was wondering if you were free after school tomorrow so you could help me out a bit with some general knowledge stuff. Dave says you're better at general knowledge than anyone he knows.'

'Really?' I said.

'Yeah,' he said. 'He reckons Mrs Parker's lining you up as Holly Hill's secret weapon.'

'Really?' I said.

'Yeah,' he said.

No pressure then.

8.30pm

Found Dad in my bedroom measuring my walls.

I said, 'Dad, I thought you were leaving the shelf thing till the weekend.'

He said, 'I am. I just wanted to measure the space. Get a feel for where they might go.'

'Right,' I said. 'While you're in here, can I ask you something?'

He said, 'Is it about your bookshelves?'

I said, 'No. It's about telling someone about God.'

That got his attention. He put his tape measure down and sat on the bed. My walls were safe. For now.

'I had this chance today to tell Tansy I'm a Christian,' I said. 'Only … I kind of didn't tell her.'

'Why's that?' Dad said.

'I didn't know how,' I said. 'I thought if I just sort of said it she might think I'm a bit of a … goody-goody. I mean, people who don't go to church have this idea about it, don't they?'

'Mmm,' Dad said, 'it's often the wrong idea. And unfortunately that gives them the wrong idea about God. That's why it's up to the ones who know what God's really like to tell the ones who don't know how fantastic He actually is – how He wants to look after us and love us and give us life that lasts for ever. If we keep it to ourselves, how's anyone ever going to find out? If we care about people, we should tell them. They need to know.'

I said, 'But supposing Tansy doesn't want to know? She was actually quite chatty today. What's she going to think of me when she knows I'm a Christian?'

Dad said, 'What do you think Jesus says when He talks with God about you? Do you think He says, "I'm not going to talk about Paul today, Father. I mean, he's not perfect, and if I talk about him You might go off me for being his friend"? Or, do you think He says, "I want to have a chat about my mate, Paul. He's made some mistakes and done a few things wrong, but he's always really sorry afterwards and I know he wants to do his best for You. Please forgive him, Father, and love him, and never let him go"?'

I didn't answer. It was kind of screamingly obvious.

'Jesus sticks up for you, doesn't He?' Dad smiled. 'Whatever you've done, however much you may have hurt Him, He never lets you down. And God never lets you down. So, really, the least we can do is try and stick up for Him too.'

'It's not that easy though, Dad, ' I said. 'Why can't it just be easy?'

'It's not easy being a Christian,' he said. 'It's fantastic and it can be very exciting, but it's not easy. And that's why, when we're having a struggle with something, we're not meant to try and deal with it on our own. We've got other Christians to help us out and we've got God. And every time we ask God to help us, we can be absolutely sure that's exactly what He'll do.'

I wonder if God could help Dad to see that I don't need bookshelves.

JESUS STICKS UP FOR ME!

HE NEVER LETS ME DOWN

COOL.

8.45pm

Dear Lord God, I'm sorry I didn't tell Tansy about going to church. I know I should have done. If I had, she might have said, 'Really? What do you go to church for?' which would have been mega because then I could have told her all about being Your friend. I could have explained to her that You want to be her friend too. I could even have invited her to come to church with me sometime. Only none of that happened because I didn't tell her. I didn't want her to know. I was thinking more about what she'd think of me than about You. I didn't stick up for You. I'm sorry. So, what I want to ask is, please could I have another go? Could there be another time to tell Tansy about You? And when it comes up, please could You help me to say all the right things? Thanks, Lord, for … well, You know, everything. Amen.

9.00pm

Only one thing's still bothering me. Nothing's changed apart from Tansy. I mean, I've still got glasses, I'm still shorter than she is. I'm never going to be tall and sporty because that's just not what I am. So why is Tansy suddenly being all buddy buddy?

WEDNESDAY 29 SEPTEMBER
6.30pm

Just got back from Benny's. Mum's been cooking again. She's made a carrot cake. She says it's an amazingly simple way to get children to eat vegetables. She's got a point. Her carrot cake's gorgeous! Think how healthy we'd all be if you could get spinach pudding, cabbage trifle and broccoli gateau. Children everywhere would be begging to eat healthily.

6.45pm

Benny's general knowledge is actually pretty good. I've lent him my book: '1001 Things All School Kids Should Know Before They're 12'. Mum found it at a car boot sale while she was rummaging about for books on how to grow a herb garden in pots, or something.

The only slightly worrying thing is that when I asked Benny what the capital of England was, he said, 'E'.

I said, 'E?'

He said, 'E.'

I said, 'That doesn't even make sense.'

He said, 'Yes, it does. E. Capital E for England.'

I said, 'No! I'm not talking about capital letters. What kind of a question would that be, anyway? What I meant was, what's the capital <u>city</u> of England?'

He said, 'Dunno … What's a capital city?'

Tragic.

7.30pm

Tansy wasn't around at lunch time today because of choir club. It was supposed to be on yesterday but Mr Mallory wasn't in school. He hasn't been in school quite a lot lately. Apparently he's got important 'teachers' courses' he has to go on, but I've got a theory about him now. I don't think he's actually a human at all. I think he's a battery-powered robot and every so often he has to stay at home so he can plug himself in to recharge. Like you do with a mobile phone.

I told Benny and he said, 'That would explain a lot. I've always thought Mr Mallory walks like a robot.'

The only time Tansy really spoke to me today was at home time. It was weird though.

She said, 'You're in a gang with Sarah, aren't you?'

I said, 'Yes. How did you know?'

She said, 'Sarah was talking about it. She says you hang out together a lot.'

'I suppose,' I said. 'I mean, the Gang hangs out together. It's not just me and Sarah.'

So maybe Tansy already knows about me and God, I thought. If Sarah's told her about the Topz Gang, she's quite likely to have told her that we're all Christians.

I waited for her to say something like, 'So what's all this about you and God?' because then I could try and say all the right things, even though, at that precise minute, I hadn't a clue what all the right things to say were. She didn't.

Very surprisingly, instead she said, 'Sarah says you're a real brainbox.'

'Does she?' I said.

'Yeah,' she said. 'She says Holly Hill can't lose the inter-school quiz challenge because you're going to be on the team.'

'Well, I'm not necessarily going to be on the team,' I said. 'I've got to get through the test on Friday first.'

'Sarah says there's no way Mrs Parker isn't going to pick you.'

'That's … nice,' I said. 'Are you going in for it?'

'Me? No!' she said. 'I'm a real dope when it comes to anything clever.'

'I bet you're not,' I said.

'I so am!' she insisted. 'I used to think the Tower of London was a pizza restaurant.'

'That's OK,' I said. 'I bet it'd make a really cool pizza restaurant.'

'Oh well, got to go,' she said. 'But at least now I know who to come to when I'm stuck on my homework.'

THURSDAY 30 SEPTEMBER

8.30pm

Just got back from Boys' Brigade. Our health and safety presentation was totally ace. Dave's a natural. He managed to talk all about how to be safe at home with the cooker and matches and plugs and all that sort of stuff <u>and</u> make it sound really interesting. Greg said we were both superstars, but basically all I did was hold up the diagrams – obviously in a superstar-ish sort of way though.

Dave has definitely got to forget this bike shop idea and think about getting a job on the telly. He's <u>made</u> for it like an octopus is made for having eight legs.

9.00pm

It won't go away. I thought that after being such a raving success at Boys' Brigade I'd have forgotten about it. I haven't. It's actually pretty amazing I was able to keep my mind on the health and safety stuff at all.

At morning break Tansy rushed up to me in the cloakroom and said, 'Paul, you've got to help me. You know those science questions we were supposed to do for this afternoon? Well, I tried, I really tried, but I don't understand a word.'

I said, 'That's OK. I'll see if I can explain it to you.'

'No!' she said. 'There isn't enough time for you to explain it to me. Anyway, I'm so dumb, I probably still wouldn't get it. But I'm sure you've got every answer right, so I'm just going to have to copy yours.'

'Copy mine?' I said. It was the last thing I was expecting.

'Yeah,' she said. 'What else?'

'It's just,' I said, 'we're not supposed to copy each other's work.'

'So?' she said. 'Who's going to know unless you tell them?'

I didn't know what to say. I didn't know what to do. No one had ever asked me anything like that before. Whatever I did, I couldn't see how it was going to be good for me. If I said yes, I'd be helping Tansy to cheat and if I said no, she'd probably never speak to me again. It was one of those 'no win' situations I've heard Dad going on about to Mum.

'Oh, come on, Paul,' she said. 'Just this one time. I <u>promise</u> I won't ask you ever again.'

I wanted to help her. It's good to help people. And I wanted Tansy to see that I'm a helpful sort of person. But what would God think about helping someone to cheat? On the other hand, if Tansy never had anything to do with me again, how would I ever get another chance to tell her about Him?

Then she had to go and say it.

'Paul, PLEEEASE! I thought you were my friend.'

'I <u>am</u> your friend,' I said.

'Then prove it. Let me copy your science.'

I got it out of my bag and gave it to her. She dashed off with it into the girls' toilets.

In science this afternoon, Mrs Parker went through the answers. She gave me and Tansy a gold star each for both getting fifteen out of fifteen.

9.15pm

Dad came in to say goodnight.

He said, 'What's up with you, then? Mum says Greg was really impressed with your health and safety presentation. I thought you'd have a head the size of a house this evening.'

'Normally I would,' I said. 'I'm just tired. And I've got arm ache. I had to hold up a lot of diagrams this evening.'

'Get a good sleep, then,' he said. 'Rest those diagram-holding arms.'

He was about to go downstairs, but I had to ask him.

'Dad, if someone needs your help, you should just give it to them, right?'

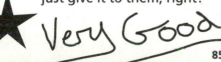

'Pretty much,' Dad said. 'We should always try to help each other where we can.'

'That's what I thought,' I said.

And that's what I've done. I could help Tansy so I did. I stopped her getting in trouble for not doing her homework. That's a good thing, isn't it? So was it really wrong letting Tansy copy my science? I know it was cheating but it was helping her too. I mean, when I get round to telling her about God and what it means to me to be His friend, she's not going to think much of me if I haven't bothered to help her. She'll say, 'For someone who's supposed to have God in his life, you're not very loving. You wouldn't help me out with that science.'

And that wouldn't make God look good either. People who don't know God need to be able to see Him in the people who <u>do</u> know Him. They need to be able to see how good and kind and wonderful He is. Then maybe they'll begin to understand how amazing it is being His friend, and they might want to get to know Him too. They're never going to want to get to know some selfish person who won't even help out with a bit of homework. That's all it was. A bit of science. Some stupid, sad questions about energy. What is the big deal here?

Anyway, Tansy promised she'd never ask if she could copy my work again. So this was just a one-off. Next time she asks for help, I'll be able to give her normal help. Non-cheating sort of help. The sort of help I KNOW God will be happy with.

I must have done the right thing.

I MUST have done ... mustn't I?

9.30pm

Dear Lord God, why is it everything to do with Tansy makes me feel bad? I even got to help her today but I still don't feel good about it. It was the right thing to help her, I know it was. It just wasn't the right sort of help. I helped her to do something wrong. Only if I hadn't, she'd have thought I was a stupid, nerdy goody-goody. She'd probably never have spoken to me again. And she'd have got into trouble. It's so hard knowing what's the right thing to do all the time. It won't happen again, though, because Tansy's not going to ask again. I mean, she might ask for help but she won't ask to copy my work. She promised. I just don't want her thinking badly about me, that's all. Amen.

9.45pm

I really wish Mrs Parker hadn't given us those gold stars.

FRIDAY 1 OCTOBER

4.30pm

She promised. Tansy PROMISED. She said she'd never ask to copy my stuff again. She must have forgotten.

5.00pm

I said to Mum, 'Would you mind if I didn't go to youth club tonight?'

She said, 'Why? Is something else happening?'

I said, 'No. I just feel like staying at home.'

She said, 'That's not like you.'

I've never understood why people say that. 'That's not like you.' How can it not be like me? It must be like me or I wouldn't have said it. I'm the one who said it. I'm the one who wants to stay at home. How can it not be like me when it's all about what I feel like doing?

HOW CAN IT NOT BE LIKE ME?

5.20pm

Greg rang.

He said, 'When you come to youth club later, would you mind bringing in that DVD you've got about dolphins?'

I said, 'Of course I wouldn't, only I don't think I'm going to be there tonight. Can I bring it next week?'

He said, 'Sure. What are you up to tonight, then?'

I said, 'Nothing special. I just feel like staying at home.'

He said (wait for it), 'That's not like you.'

HUMPH!

5.50pm

I was upstairs when I heard Dad come in. The whole street probably heard Dad come in. He crashed loudly through the front door and yelled, 'Hellooo, peoples! Sorry I'm late.'

He's normally quite loud and excited on a Friday because it's the weekend, but this was definitely louder and more excited than usual. It must be the whizzy-dizzying thought of being able to spend the entire day tomorrow putting up shelves. I mean, whoop-de-doo.

Then I heard Dad say to Mum, 'Paul all ready for youth club? We're going to have to get our skates on or we'll be late.'

Mum said, 'Oh, it's all right. He doesn't want to go this evening.'

Dad said, 'Doesn't he?'

Mum said, 'No, he doesn't. Says he feels like staying at home.'

'Odd,' said Dad. 'THAT'S NOT LIKE PAUL.'

6.00pm

So, what is Paul like? Everyone thinks they know so much about him. **WHAT IS HE REALLY LIKE?**

6.15pm

I used to think I knew myself inside out, back to front, upside down and round the bend. I mean, I live with myself every day, don't I? No one can know me better than I do. It stands to reason.

So why have I done what I've done? Again. I didn't stand up for myself. I didn't stand up for God. I just gave in.

At home time Tansy said, 'I'm never going to be able to do that maths sheet Mrs Parker gave us. I can hardly divide up a cake let alone numbers. You do it and I'll copy yours on Monday.'

And what did I say?

I said, 'OK.'

8.45pm

Benny rang.

He said, 'Where were you this evening?'

I said, 'Here. Where d'you think I was?'

He said, 'I don't know, do I? That's why I'm asking.'

I said, 'Well, now you do know.'

He said, 'Right. Anyway, you bombed off so fast I didn't get a chance to talk to you after the quiz test this afternoon. How did it go?'

'OK, I think,' I said.

'I think mine went OK too,' Benny said. 'I managed to answer most of it. There was one tricky question, though. Which country's the leaning tower of Pisa in?'

'Italy,' I said.

'Are you sure?' he said.

'Positive,' I said.

'Oh,' he said.

'Why?' I said. 'What did you put?'

'Scotland,' he said.

'Oh well,' I said, 'Mrs Parker won't be expecting us to get every question right.'

'That's good,' he said, 'because you know the chocolate one?'

'You mean, what kind of bean is used to make chocolate?'

'That's the one,' he said.

'What did you put?' I said.

'A really nice bean.'

'It's a cocoa bean, you dipstick.'

'I know that <u>now</u>,' he said. 'I looked it up in your book. Anyway, when do we find out if we're in the quiz?'

'Tuesday, I think,' I said.

'Cool,' he said. 'So, why weren't you at youth club?'

'I just wasn't,' I said.

'Dave's right, isn't he?' he said. 'There is something up with you.'

'What do you mean?' I said.

'Dave says you seem funny.'

'Thanks. Look, there's nothing "up with me", OK? Anyway I've got to go. Mum's just made hot chocolate. With really nice beans.'

9.15pm

Phone went. Mum's usually pretty cool and calm when she's talking on the phone – even that time Dad rang on her birthday to say he couldn't take her out after all because he'd just run out of petrol in the middle of nowhere, and wouldn't be home for at least three hours.

Not this time though. She started shrieking. Mum never shrieks.

'No! You're joking! Right now? Oooooh!'

Spooky or what?

I decided to stay in my bedroom. There are definitely times when it's best to give parents some personal space.

Obviously there are other times when personal space is the last thing they want – as I realised when Mum then burst into my room and threw her arms around me in a rather disturbing sort of major huggy thing. Dad was right behind her, grinning.

'That was Uncle Will,' Mum said, all out of breath as

if she'd had to run halfway round Holly
to find me. 'Auntie Jo-Jo's having her
baby!' (I wish they wouldn't keep calling
her Auntie Jo-Jo. I used to call her Auntie
Jo-Jo when I was three. I mean, hello? I've
moved on since then. Can't we just drop a 'Jo'?)

'I know Auntie <u>Jo's</u> having a baby,' I said pointedly.
'We've known for months.'

'No!' said Mum. 'She's HAVING her baby. Now! This
minute! It's being born!'

9.30pm
Wow. That is kind of a wow thing actually. Auntie Jo's
having her baby. Right now. This very second in world
history. Brand new person on the way. I'm about to be a
cousin. **Cool.**

SATURDAY 2 OCTOBER
7.00am
If I'd been asleep, I might have been in a major moody-
poody at being woken up at half-past six this morning
by the sound of Dad making a sort of strangled sound
as he hurtled towards me in his baggy old pyjamas,
slurping a cup of tea. As I was wide awake, it didn't
make a lot of difference. I'd been awake for ages.
Thinking. Worrying. About Tansy. No surprises there,
then. At least Dad managed to avoid throwing his tea at
me when he tripped over my rug – which he seemed to
find mind-bendingly hilarious.

'Get yourself up,' he said when he was actually able
to speak again without bursting into fits of giggles and
spitting tea everywhere. (And he has the nerve to call

me childish.) 'We're off to Hampshire.'

Of course! Auntie Jo's baby. She's arrived apparently.

They're calling her Mollie Rose. Wicked. Sounds
a bit like a ship. The Mollie Rose. I can imagine
her being launched at a huge ceremony by
someone terribly famous and wearing a big
hat.

Oh, flying fishcakes, what is the matter
with me? I really must get more sleep.

8.45am

I'm sitting in the car with Mum. We kind of juddered to
a halt about a quarter of an hour ago.

'Ah,' Dad said.

'What is it?' said Mum.

'Petrol,' said Dad. 'We've run out.'

I wonder why Dad seems to wait for the really
important journeys to run out of petrol. Mum was not
happy.

'There's a petrol station not far from here,' Dad said.
'We can walk to it and get a can full. It won't take long.'

'We are not walking anywhere,' Mum said. 'You're
the one who's run out of petrol. You're the one who
can go and find some.'

'Right,' Dad said.

'Exactly,' Mum replied. 'And get a move on, please. There's a baby waiting to be cuddled.'

Dad glanced at me.

'Paul?' he said, by which I think he meant, 'Do you fancy a walk to the petrol station?' as if he was offering me some kind of once-in-a-lifetime opportunity.

'No, it's OK,' I said. 'I'll stay with Mum.'

Glad I brought my diary. Glad I <u>didn't</u> bring my maths homework.

9.00am

Still no sign of Dad. Mum's just opened a packet of chocolate fingers. She says it's a long time since breakfast.

I said, 'Mum, if someone asked you to do something for them to help them out, but it was actually a bad thing, would you do it anyway? You know, because it was helping them?'

She said, 'That's a big question for a Saturday morning.'

I said, 'Would you, though? After all, God wants us to help people, doesn't He?'

She said, 'If someone wants you to do something that's bad then it can't really be good for them, can it? And if it's not good, it's not helpful. We help people when we do good things for them. That's what God wants.'

I said, 'It's a good thing to help friends with their homework, though, isn't it?'

'Of course it is,' she said.

'Yeah, that's what I thought,' I said.

'As long as you don't end up actually doing it for them.'

'Right.'

'Just doing it for them isn't helping them learn, is it?'

'No.'

'So that would be a bad thing, wouldn't it?'

'Yes.'

I noticed she was looking at me over the top of her glasses. She does that when she's thinking – like Greg does his chewy-lip thing.

'Does this have anything to do with you not going to youth club?' she asked.

'No,' I said.

'Mmm,' she said. 'You'd better have another chocolate finger then.'

9.10am

That's it, isn't it? I mean, it's obvious. The best way to help Tansy is <u>not</u> to help her. Not in the way she wants anyway. I'm doing my maths tomorrow and I'm not letting anyone in the whole, wide, ENTIRE world copy it. Not even if they're from America. Never, never. Not for anything.

NOT EVER.

9.20am

At last. Dad's back. We're off again. It's amazing how much better the car goes when it's got petrol in it. Brrrm, brrrm.

Brrrm   Brrrm   Brrrm

7.00pm

When you see someone else's baby, it's hard to imagine you were ever like that yourself. I know I must have been a baby once because Mum and Dad have got the photos to prove it. I was very sort of round and bald. Mollie Rose isn't bald. She's got quite a lot of curly blonde hair. Mum kept saying, 'Just look at those gorgeous, blonde curls,' over and over again, as if we might not have spotted them or something.

Other than the blonde bit, Mollie's quite pink. Pink and shrivelled. If I was pink and shrivelled, people would go, 'Bleeeahh!' but it's actually quite cute in a baby.

Mum said, 'It doesn't seem five minutes since you were that size.'

I said, 'It does to me.'

She said, 'That's only because you don't remember it like I do.'

I thought, I'm glad I don't remember it really. It must be so mind-crunchingly boring being stuck lying about in a cot for most of the day, not to mention having to put up with being handed round from grown-up to grown-up so that they can cuddle you and go all gooey just because you happen to be small and gurgly. I mean, it's not as if you can get up and muck around on your website or invent something. It's all nappies and baby cream and sludgy-looking food.

That's how it looks to me anyway. I think it'll be OK for Mollie Rose, though. She looks as if she's going to enjoy being a baby. And she's not a bit like a ship.

Before we went home, I leaned over that see-through, plastic cot thing she was lying in at the hospital and said, 'Bye, Mollie Rose. You're a cool baby. Welcome to the planet.'

Then we actually managed to get all the way back to Holly Hill without running out of petrol. Good one, Dad.

8.00pm

Just done my maths homework. Decimals. I like decimals. When Tansy asks to copy it on Monday, I'm going to say no.

9.00pm

Dear Lord God, Mum says we need to say thank you that Mollie Rose arrived safely, so thank You. And thank You for all her pink shrivelled-upness. When Jesus came to earth, He was just a baby. I wonder if He was pink and shrivelled like Mollie Rose, or more round and bald like me. Mum says a brand new life is a miracle. I suppose it is really. And being brand new is ... well ... as new as it's possible to be. Mum says that's the incredible thing about being Your friend. We don't stay new babies, but because You're always ready to forgive us when we do things wrong, it's as if we have a brand new life every day. A clean life. A life that's full of You, which is the best sort of life to have. All we have to do is say sorry and the bad things are washed away.

So thank You for my brand new baby cousin. And thank You for my brand new life. I'm sorry about the homework-copying thing. I'm sorry I tried to pretend it was the right thing to do when I knew all along it wasn't, it was just cheating. I won't let it happen again. I'll talk to Tansy on Monday. She'll understand. She'll have to. Amen.

SUNDAY 3 OCTOBER
9.30am

Dad was munching on cornflakes. He doesn't have milk. Just cornflakes.

I said, 'Dad, I've just realised. Feeling guilty's horrible, but in some ways it can be a good thing.'

'How do you mean?' Dad munched.

I said, 'I reckon feeling guilty is God's way of telling us we've done something wrong.'

'I reckon you could be right,' Dad munched. 'Have you been feeling guilty, then?'

'Yes,' I said. 'I was trying to make something seem all right, but it just wasn't. And the more right I tried to make it in my head, the more it was all wrong.'

'Do you want to tell me a bit more?'

'I don't think I need to. I've told God and I've said sorry. Now all I've got to do is the right thing.'

'Great,' said Dad. 'Glad I was able to help.'

You see? Sorted. I'm done with doing the wrong thing because of Tansy. I'm done with feeling guilty and God's forgiven me. I've got a brand new life again.

I reckon feeling guilty is God's way of telling us we've done something wrong.

4.00pm

Been to the park playing footie with Danny, Benny and Josie. I was in goal. Josie says she likes it when I'm in goal because she gets to score a lot.

I said, 'OK, so maybe I let the odd one sneak past me, but if God had made everyone good at football, there'd be no one left to invent things.'

'Good point,' said Danny. 'I bet you'll be a world famous professor-type person one day.'

'Yeah,' said Benny. 'You'll probably do something really mega cool like invent some kind of car that doesn't need petrol – you know, to help stop global warming and all that.'

'Er, Benny,' I said kindly, 'someone's already invented a car that doesn't need petrol. It's electric.'

'Have they?' he said. 'Oh well, maybe you could come up with the very first non-petrol, non-electric, non-anything-bad-for-the-world type of thing for getting you around.'

'Benny,' I said, 'it's already out there. It's called a bike.'

'All right, smarty-glasses,' he said and kicked the ball past me so fast I didn't even see it, putting his score at about 297.

It was all going great. Then all of a sudden Tansy appeared. She was with her mum. They were walking a dog.

'I didn't know you had a dog,' said Josie.

'We only got her yesterday,' said Tansy, 'from the rescue centre.'

'What's her name?' said Josie.

'Sheba,' said Tansy, 'and she's all mine.'

'She's gorgeous,' said Josie.

I didn't know what to do. How to be. I wasn't expecting to see Tansy. Not till tomorrow. I kind of knew what I had to say to her but I wasn't ready to say it. Not today. Anyway her mum was right there. I definitely couldn't say anything in front of her mum.

I thought, maybe they won't stop. After all, they've got to take Sheba for a walk. Dogs don't like to be kept waiting. That's what John always says about Gruff.

'I'm going to take Sheba over by the trees,' said Tansy's mum. 'Stay here with your friends if you want.'

On the other hand, maybe Tansy would stop and I'd just have to talk to her today.

'OK,' said Tansy. 'I need to have a chat with Paul "the brains" anyway.'

I should have been pleased. All-American Tansy called

me 'the brains'. All-American Tansy wanted to talk to me. Trouble is, I knew exactly what she wanted to talk to me about.

'Actually, I was just in goal,' I said.

'Don't worry,' said Josie. 'I'll do it for a bit.'

She was gone before I could stop her.

Tansy waited till the others were far enough away not to hear.

Then she said, 'So, brainbox, did you do the maths?'

'Yeah,' I said.

'Great,' she said. 'I'll get it from you in the morning. Wait for me in the cloakroom.'

'The thing is … it's just …'

'What?' she said, 'You're not going to let me down, are you? There's nothing to worry about. No one found out about the science.'

'I know,' I said. 'It … doesn't mean it's the right thing to do, though.'

'Yes, it does,' she said. 'The right thing is to help people who are your friends. And I'm one of your friends, aren't I, Paul?'

'Yes.'

'Then you'll help me out, won't you, and that way we'll stay friends. Won't we?'

That's exactly it. That's the only reason she is my 'friend'. So she can copy my work.

4.30pm

I thought I could tell her. I thought I'd be able to say it. But I couldn't. Not when she was standing there looking at me.

I just couldn't.

'Aren't you going back in goal?' Danny said, when Tansy had gone.

'No,' I said. 'I think I'm going to go home.'

'What for?' said Josie. 'I won't score half so many times if you're not here. And that means Benny'll win. Again.'

'So?' I snapped. 'He'll just have to win then, won't he?'

I ran out of the park. They must think I'm such a loser. The worst part is they're probably right.

6.00pm

'Paul,' Mum called. 'Danny's here for you.'

We went up to my room.

'What was all that about in the park?' Danny said. 'Josie was only messing around. You're not <u>that</u> bad at keeping goal.'

'Actually, I am,' I said.

'Come on, though,' he said, 'you don't normally storm off like that. What's up?'

'Nothing. And anyway, if anything is, it's <u>my</u> problem and I'm the one who's got to sort it out.'

'Something does need sorting out, then,' Danny said.

'Yeah,' I said.

'So, <u>what is it</u>?'

He obviously wasn't going to let it drop.

'It's Tansy, all right?' I muttered.

'I worked <u>that</u> out already,' he said, 'but what about her?'

I told him. I told him how everything should be really cool now because all of a sudden she seemed to want to be my best friend. Then I told him why.

'She only "likes" me because she wants to get to copy my homework all the time.'

'But you're not going to let her, are you?' said Danny.

'That's just it,' I said. 'I <u>did</u> let her. Last week. And I've told God I'm sorry because I am, I really am, but she wants to copy my maths tomorrow and I don't know how to tell her she can't. I thought it'd be easy – you know, "You're not copying it!" Only I couldn't say it. When I saw her, I just couldn't say it.'

'Mmm,' said Danny.

After a minute he asked, 'Is it difficult to tell her because you don't want to let her down or because you think she won't want to be your friend any more?'

I shrugged.

'It's because you think she won't want to be your friend any more, isn't it?' he said.

'Well, wouldn't you feel like that? I mean, who <u>wants</u> someone not to be their friend any more?'

'Mmm,' Danny said again.

Then he said, 'Shall I tell you what Greg said to me once? Greg said you can't spend all your time worrying about what other people are going to think of you if you do what you know is right. You've got to think about God first and do what <u>He'd</u> want you to do. God wouldn't want you to help Tansy cheat, would He?'

'No,' I said.

'And even if she does end up falling out with you over it, it's more important to do what God says than what Tansy says. Isn't it?'

I nodded. I was quite shocked actually. I had no idea Danny could be so … wise. Imagine being wise and super fit.

'I know what God wants me to do,' I said, 'and

I know what I've got to tell Tansy. I just don't seem to know how.'

'Well,' said Danny, 'maybe you need someone to tell her with you.'

'Who's going to do that?' I said. 'No one knows apart from you.'

'It'll have to be me then, won't it? Duh!'

6.30pm
I can't get over it. I really let Danny down a few weeks ago when he asked me to go swimming with him and I made out to Tansy that I hated the whole idea. Now he wants to help me. I mean, he could easily have said, 'It's your problem, you deal with it, cheater.' I wouldn't have blamed him.

But he didn't.

He said, 'Shall we pray about it?'

DANNY'S PRAYER

Lord, it's so easy to do the wrong thing. It's so easy to worry more about what other people will think of us than about what You want us to do. Help us to explain to Tansy tomorrow why Paul can't let her copy his homework. Help her to understand that it's not because he's being mean but because he wants to help her in the right way and not in the wrong way. And help us to be able to show her how much we love You and how important it is to be Your friends. Amen.

PRAYER PRAYER PRAYER PRAYER

6.40pm
Wow. That's all I can say.

6.50pm
Really.

Wow.

MONDAY 4 OCTOBER

6.45am

PRESS-UPS AND PORRIDGE ...

Dear Lord God, I'm so SCARED. What happens if I get to school and Danny won't help me after all? What happens if he does help me and Tansy says she hates both of us and she's never going to speak to us again? What happens if she says she never wanted anything to do with a nerdy nerd like me in the first place? What if it all goes horribly wrong and she thinks I'm just a goody-goody creep and tells the whole of Holly Hill Primary what a total loser I am? How am I ever going to be able to eat breakfast feeling like this? Help! Please!

6.50am

I don't think I can do this.

I just don't think I can do this.

7.00am

Mum said, 'Of course you can't ring Danny. It's seven o'clock in the morning.'

I said, 'I know. But it's a school day. He's probably been awake for an hour doing press-ups or something in his bedroom.'

'No,' said Mum.

'Pleeeease!' I said.

'No!' said Mum. 'Why do you need to talk to him at seven o'clock in the morning?'

'I just do,' I said. 'Pleeeeease!'

She was doing the looking-at-me-over-her-glasses thing.

'What's the matter, Paul?' she asked. 'What's the problem?'

'I just need to talk to him, that's all. It's about something he's going to help me with today.'

She was still looking at me. Then –

'Oh, all right,' she sighed. 'You can ring him quickly at eight o'clock. And not a minute before.'

Phew! Right. That gives me an hour. What can I do for an hour?

I know. Press-ups.

7.05am

I'll never understand why people do press-ups. How can anything that hurts that much be good for you? I mean, press-ups are supposed to help make your arms strong and build up muscles. Maybe they only build up muscles if you've actually <u>GOT</u> muscles to build up. Obviously I haven't and that's why they hurt so much.

7.10am

Mum knocked on the door.

She said, 'I'm making you some porridge. If something important's happening at school today, you're going to need a good breakfast.'

What Mum doesn't realise is that what I need and what I'm going to be able to eat are two completely different things this morning.

Mind you, we haven't had porridge for ages …

7.45am

Dad had porridge too. It was just me and him in the kitchen.

'Sorry I didn't get round to putting up your shelves in the end,' he said.

'Doesn't matter,' I said.

'Still,' he said, 'it was great going to meet baby Mollie, wasn't it? And anyway, we're not shooting off anywhere next weekend. I can put up a few for you then, eh?'

'Yeah,' I said.

'So,' he said, 'what's this Mum says about you needing to make an important phone call to Danny?'

I knew it. The porridge thing was all part of a clever plan to get me to talk.

'Oh, it's nothing.'

'Doesn't sound like nothing,' Dad said. 'You've been quiet all weekend.'

'The thing is,' I said, 'it's just … I mean, it's like … I can't really … Oh, it's just school sort of stuff … You know …'

'And this "school sort of stuff" is really worrying you, is it?' Dad said.

I nodded. (It's all I could do. My mouth was all stuck up with porridge.)

'Anything I can help with?' he asked.

'No,' I gulped. 'There's just something I've got to do.'

He didn't say anything straightaway. (<u>His</u> mouth was all stuck up with porridge.)

'Whatever it is,' he said eventually, 'God'll be right there with you. You do know that, don't you?'

'Yes,' I said. 'It's just that sometimes, when you're <u>really</u> worried, the worry can seem bigger than God.'

'No worry is ever bigger than God,' Dad said. 'He's enormous! In the Bible we're told to give all our worries and cares to Him and He'll make us strong enough to deal with them. Say to Him, "Lord God, You know what my big worry is. Please help me to cope with it and to know that You're with me all the way."'

I said, 'It's hard to do that with a big worry, though.'

'I know it's hard,' Dad said. 'It means you really have to trust Him. But if you ask Him, Paul, He'll be there. That's what He's promised. And God always keeps His promises.'

No worry is ever bigger than God

Trust Trust
Promise Promise

7.55am

OK, Lord, this is it. You know what I've got to do. You know how scary it is. I've never been any good at standing up to people. Maybe it's because I'm shorter than people like Danny. And Tansy. But You love me, I know You do. You made me just the way I am, glasses and everything. You've got this huge purpose for me. You've given me a brand new life and no one can take any of that away. So, please help me to talk to Tansy this morning and, however she feels about me afterwards, help me to know that it doesn't matter. What's important is that I'll have done the right thing, not the wrong thing, and every time I do the right thing, it means I'm standing up for You. I'm going to trust You, Lord. I've decided. Amen.

And by the way, thanks for Mum and Dad. They're cool – even if they can be a bit crazy sometimes.

8.10am

Mum asked, 'Aren't you going to go and ring Danny?'

'Nah,' I said. 'Thought I'd talk it over with God instead.'

4.30pm

Got to school. Danny was already in the cloakroom. He'd asked his mum to drop him off a bit early to make sure he was there in time. Macaroonies! I mean, how good a friend is that.

'Thanks, Danny,' I said.

'No probs,' he said. 'You'd do the same for me.'

Would I? I thought. I hope I would. I'd make sure I would.

'The thing is, Danny,' I said, 'I had this chat with Dad

over porridge. I didn't really want a chat. I didn't really want porridge, come to that. But actually they both turned out to be pretty good.'

'Did they?' Danny said. 'Don't really like porridge.'

'Anyway,' I said, 'Dad says no worry is bigger than God.'

'Did you know that in Scotland they eat it with salt on?' Danny said.

'And if God's bigger than all the worries I'm ever going to have, then He'll help me to cope with them.'

'I think I did have it with golden syrup once, which was OK,' Danny said, 'but I suppose it's just not really my thing.'

'So, what I'm trying to say is,' I said, 'it's really great of you to want to help me and everything, I mean really, REALLY great, but ... I think this is something I've got to do on my own – or rather, not on my own, but with God. Me and God. Do you understand?'

Danny did understand. He even said he thought that was a much better idea. He's going to meet me at break to find out what happened. He is definitely one mega cool dude.

So there we were in the cloakroom. God and me. Waiting.

It wasn't just God and me the whole time, obviously. Everyone was arriving for school, so the cloakroom was quite busy. All I could do was hang around near my peg.

Funny thing was, there was no sign of Tansy. The registration bell went. There was <u>still</u> no sign of Tansy. Was she coming or wasn't she coming? Maybe she was pretending to be ill so she could stay at home in case I didn't let her have my maths. Maybe she really <u>was</u> ill. Maybe she'd caught some nasty bug that only made you ill if you came from America. Maybe …

No. There she was.

She brushed right past me. Didn't even say hello.

All she did say was, 'Can't talk now. Too late. Stupid car wouldn't start. Be in here at break.'

Then she was gone again. A bit like a puff of smoke. Without the funny smell.

5.00pm

Mum just called me downstairs. She's gone all gooey again. Uncle Will's emailed through all these photos of Mollie Rose.

'Isn't she just such a little cutesy-pie?' she keeps saying.

Good job Dad's not home yet otherwise he'd be at it too.

Not that Mollie <u>isn't</u> a cutesy-pie baby, I don't mean that. She's actually huge in the cutesy-pie department. It's just that having both your parents all gooey at the same time can be a bit, well, tiring.

Awww cute

couchy-couchy-coo!

Ga-Ga

5.05pm

So where was I? Oh yeah, Tansy being like a puff of smoke.

Come to think of it, Tansy was probably a cutesy-pie baby too. I bet she was always being gooed over and having her photo taken, and she was probably in all the local 'Beautiful Baby' competitions (if they have them in America). Mum never put me in for one of those. She says she didn't need to enter me in some silly contest to know how beautiful I was – which is pretty gooey but definitely nice. Especially as I was round and bald.

Danny shot over to me at break.

'What happened?' he said.

'Nothing yet,' I said. 'I'm going to meet her now.' I felt a bit like some kind of secret agent.

I went right to the cloakroom and waited. Tansy didn't turn up straight away. I thought I might as well eat my chocolate biscuit. After all, it was sitting in my lunch box, waiting to be eaten. This turned out to be a mistake. I mean, I should have known better. If anyone in the whole school was going to walk in when my mouth was stuffed full of chocolate biscuit, it would be Tansy.

And she did. Just like with the flapjack. It's as if she has some built-in radar that says, 'OK! His mouth is full right now. Go, go, go!'

'Hi,' she said.

'Fuff,' I replied. (Oh, peanuts! I was talking gibberish to her again but what else was I supposed to say with a mouthful of biscuit?)

Tansy didn't seem to notice.

Fuff
Fuf

She just asked, 'Have you got it?'

I managed to swallow what was left of my biscuit but I still couldn't speak properly until I'd had a gulp of blackcurrant.

'Yes, I've got it,' I said finally. 'Well, when I say I've got it, I mean, I did it over the weekend, but …'

Go on, just tell her. Please help me, Lord, just to tell her!

'I did do it over the weekend, Tansy, but … I've already given it in to Mrs Parker.'

There was this horrible silence. Tansy was staring at me. Her face looked more and more angry. If anyone else had come into the cloakroom at that moment, I don't think either of us would have noticed. And I've no idea why, but I found myself thinking, I SO hope I haven't got chocolate biscuit round my mouth.

Then it came. All that anger started whooshing out.

'How could you do that, Paul? How could you do that to me? What am I going to do? You said I could copy it! You promised!'

113

'No, I didn't!' I whooshed back. 'I didn't promise anything. You're the one who promised. You copied my science and then you promised never to ask to copy anything again. If anyone's broken a promise, it's you.'

'There was me thinking you were my friend when all you are is just a stupid <u>little</u> boy!'

'No, I'm not, Tansy, and I <u>am</u> your friend!' All the right words were suddenly in my mouth. I just opened it and out they came!

'Friends want to help each other,' I said. 'Friends want to do the right thing for each other.

IT'S NOT THE RIGHT THING TO HELP YOU TO CHEAT.

If you want me to help you with your homework, then I'll help you. I'll try and explain it so you can understand. But I can't let you copy what I've done. It's wrong and I can't help you do what's wrong.'

She was standing there with her mouth open. I still had to say the most important bit.

'Tansy,' I said, 'you don't know this about me because I haven't told you yet and I should have done, but ... my best friend is God. God's always there for me. He never lets me down. But if I help you to do the wrong thing, then I'm letting <u>Him</u> down. And I can't. I just can't.'

There was another silence. Worse than the first one.

She hates me, I thought.

Her mouth suddenly snapped shut with a sort of 'humph' sound, and she turned and started to flounce out of the cloakroom.

When she got to the door, she stopped just long enough to whip round and snarl, 'And DON'T call me Tansy! I hate it when people call me Tansy. It's Taz, all right? I like it when people call me TAZ!'

TAZ TAZ TAZ

Woah! For a minute I couldn't move. Then I sat down with a bump. It was a big bump as it turned out. I'd forgotten that Mr Mallory had moved the benches. The floor was a long way down. Next thing I knew, Danny was peering at me.

'Maybe "How did it go?" isn't a good question to ask right now,' he said.

'No, no,' I said, 'it's an OK question.'

'OK,' he said. 'How did it go?'

'I told her,' I said.

'And?' Danny said.

'She hates me.'

TUESDAY 5 OCTOBER

7.30am

Lord God, I don't want to go to school today. It's not nice when someone's not speaking to you. I'll have to get used to it though because Tansy will probably never speak to me again. I know I've done the right thing and I know that You and me, we're cool, but does this mean Tansy's going to hate me for ever or will she get over it and start calling me a brainbox again? Of course she won't. She was only interested in my brainboxiness because she wanted to be able to copy my work. Thank You that at least she didn't get in trouble over that maths yesterday and Mrs Parker was really nice about it. And thank You for helping me speak up for You. I'm glad Tansy knows I'm on Your team now. Amen.

4.30pm

Sarah sat next to me on the bus home.

She said, 'Wow, Paul, you've been really brave.'

I said, 'Have I?'

'Yeah!' she said. 'You told Taz about being a Christian.'

'How do you know?' I said.

'She told me,' she said.

'Did she also tell you she hates me?' I said.

'She doesn't hate you,' Sarah said. 'She started to say something about it all, telling me what a weirdo you were, but I said to her you're not weird at all. And then I told her that I'm a Christian too, and Josie and Dave and Benny and Danny and John. I told her that that's what we're all about in the Topz Gang.'

'Oh,' I said.

'I even told her God really wanted to be her friend too and all she had to do was ask Him.'

'Really?' I said.

'Really,' she said. 'I could never have done that if it hadn't been for what you said to her.'

'Right,' I said. (I was so amazed I could only seem to get out one word at a time.)

'I know she's not talking to you at the moment,' Sarah went on, 'but I think she will talk to you again. And I think she might ask you stuff about God because she said, "God obviously really matters to Paul," as if she couldn't understand why, but sort of wanted to know.'

'Wow,' I said. (Yup. Still just one word at a time.)

When we got off the bus, Sarah said, 'Glad you got in the quiz challenge. Knew you would, though. Everyone did.'

Benny didn't get picked in the end, but he was fine about it.

He said to me, 'You've got a brainy person's brain. I've got footballers' legs. Fair's fair.'

6.30pm

Dad said, 'Everything all right at school? Did Tansy speak to you?'

'No,' I said. 'She spoke to Sarah, though. I think she might get to be one of God's friends one day.'

'You'll have to pray for her,' Dad said.

'Yes, I will,' I said. 'After all, it doesn't really matter what she thinks of me. But it does matter what she thinks of God.'

7.00pm

Dear Lord God, thank You that because You're bigger than our biggest worries, You can sort them out and turn them into something good. Thank You for helping me tell Tansy about You and thank You for helping Sarah to stand up for You too. It's hard doing things when we feel as if we're on our own, but somehow, when we talk to You, You help us to be strong enough to do what's right. Thank You for making me strong enough with Tansy. Please help her to find out more about You so that one day she'll want to be Your friend too. Amen.

8.00pm

I've just been adding some stuff to my website. I haven't done anything on my computer for days. In fact, I don't feel as if I've done anything about anything for days because all I've been doing is thinking about this Tansy business. I don't reckon I need to keep thinking about it any more. Whatever Tansy feels about me, I'm all right with it. I really am this time. It doesn't matter. Because I'm all right with God. Properly all right. And being all right with God means everything's going to be hunky. Hunky dunky even.

8.15pm

I remember Greg saying once that when we do the right thing for God, God gives us peace. I reckon that's what I've got now: peace.

8.30pm

You know what, I think I feel like inventing something. I haven't done that for ages. I wonder if Mum would fancy letting me have one of her saucepans …

Topz Secret Diaries hit the balance between humour and insightful truth as they bring well-loved *Topz* characters to life.

JOSIE'S JAZZY JOURNAL

We find out what happens when the Topz Gang's Josie meets Gabby. Josie has always felt as though she belongs – to her mum and dad, to the Topz Gang and to God – but Gabby has never felt this. So Josie, with the help of best friend Sarah, tries to show her God's love.
ISBN: 978-1-85345-457-8
£5.49

SARAH'S SECRET SCRIBBLINGS

Join Sarah from the Topz Gang as she records how she learns to pray for people who upset her, discovers that everyone is special to God and practises waiting patiently for God to answer her prayers. Packed full of laughs, smiles, advice and encouragement.
ISBN: 978-1-85345-432-5
£4.99

BENNY'S BARMY BITS

Find out just what goes on in Benny's mind and how God fits into his life. Discover with Benny, amongst other things, how God wants to be the most important part of our lives. Enjoy side-splittingly funny and exciting bits as you learn from the thought-provoking bits.
ISBN: 978-1-85345-431-8
£4.99

Prices correct at time of printing

IF YOU LIKED THIS BOOK, YOU'LL LOVE THESE:

TOPZ

An exciting, day-by-day look at the Bible for children aged from 7 to 11. As well as simple prayers and Bible readings every day, each issue includes word games, puzzles, cartoons and contributions from readers. Fun and colourful, *Topz* helps children get to know God.
ISSN: 0967-1307
£2.25 each (bimonthly)
£12.50 UK annual subscription (six issues)

TOPZ FOR NEW CHRISTIANS

Thirty days of Bible notes to help 7- to 11-year-olds find faith in Jesus and have fun exploring their new life with Him.
ISBN: 978-1-85345-104-1
£2.49

TOPZ GUIDE TO THE BIBLE

A guide offering exciting and stimulating ways for 7- to 11-year-olds to become familiar with God's Word. With a blend of colourful illustrations, cartoons and lively writing, this is the perfect way to encourage children to get to know their Bibles.
ISBN: 978-1-85345-313-7
£2.49

Prices correct at time of printing

National Distributors

UK: (and countries not listed below)
CWR, Waverley Abbey House, Waverley Lane, Farnham, Surrey GU9 8EP.
Tel: (01252) 784700 Outside UK (44) 1252 784700

AUSTRALIA: CMC Australasia, PO Box 519, Belmont, Victoria 3216.
Tel: (03) 5241 3288 Fax: (03) 5241 3290

CANADA: David C Cook Distribution Canada, PO Box 98, 55 Woodslee
Avenue, Paris, Ontario N3L 3E5. Tel: 1800 263 2664

GHANA: Challenge Enterprises of Ghana, PO Box 5723, Accra.
Tel: (021) 222437/223249 Fax: (021) 226227

HONG KONG: Cross Communications Ltd, 1/F, 562A Nathan Road,
Kowloon. Tel: 2780 1188 Fax: 2770 6229

INDIA: Crystal Communications, 10-3-18/4/1, East Marredpalli,
Secunderabad – 500026, Andhra Pradesh. Tel/Fax: (040) 27737145

KENYA: Keswick Books and Gifts Ltd, PO Box 10242, Nairobi.
Tel: (02) 331692/226047 Fax: (02) 728557

MALAYSIA: Salvation Book Centre (M) Sdn Bhd, 23 Jalan SS 2/64,
47300 Petaling Jaya, Selangor.
Tel: (03) 78766411/78766797 Fax: (03) 78757066/78756360

NEW ZEALAND: CMC Australasia, PO Box 303298, North Harbour,
Auckland 0751. Tel: 0800 449 408 Fax: 0800 449 049

NIGERIA: FBFM, Helen Baugh House, 96 St Finbarr's College Road, Akoka,
Lagos. Tel: (01) 7747429/4700218/825775/827264

PHILIPPINES: OMF Literature Inc, 776 Boni Avenue, Mandaluyong City.
Tel: (02) 531 2183 Fax: (02) 531 1960

SINGAPORE: Alby Commercial Enterprises Pte Ltd, 95 Kallang Avenue
#04-00, AIS Industrial Building, 339420.
Tel: (65) 629 27238 Fax: (65) 629 27235

SOUTH AFRICA: Struik Christian Books, 80 MacKenzie Street, PO Box 1144,
Cape Town 8000. Tel: (021) 462 4360 Fax: (021) 461 3612

SRI LANKA: Christombu Publications (Pvt) Ltd, Bartleet House,
65 Braybrooke Place, Colombo 2. Tel: (9411) 2421073/2447665

TANZANIA: CLC Christian Book Centre, PO Box 1384, Mkwepu Street,
Dar es Salaam. Tel/Fax: (022) 2119439

USA: David C Cook Distribution Canada, PO Box 98, 55 Woodslee Avenue,
Paris, Ontario N3L 3E5, Canada. Tel: 1800 263 2664

ZIMBABWE: Word of Life Books (Pvt) Ltd, Christian Media Centre,
8 Aberdeen Road, Avondale, PO Box A480 Avondale, Harare.
Tel: (04) 333355 or 091301188

For email addresses, visit the CWR website: www.cwr.org.uk

CWR is a Registered Charity – Number 294387
CWR is a Limited Company registered in England – Registration Number 1990308